"Tony?"

"Hmm?"

"Doesn't this bother you?"

"What?"

"Lying so close like this?"

"What do you mean, 'bother'?"

"I just think that since this bed is so big, we could probably lie far enough apart that we wouldn't have to touch."

"That's true."

"Wouldn't you rest better that way?"

"No doubt."

She raised her head and tried to push away from him by placing her hands on his chest. Since his mother hadn't raised a fool, Tony left his arms around her. She was firmly anchored to his side by his leg still across hers.

Christina brushed her hand across his chest in a smooth caress that made him want to purr. "Don't you want to rest?" she finally asked.

"Not particularly."

Dear Reader,

This month's lineup is so exciting, I don't know where to start...so I guess I'll just "take it from the top" with our October *MAN OF THE MONTH*. *Temptation Texas Style!* by Annette Broadrick is a long-awaited addition to her SONS OF TEXAS series. I know you won't want to miss this continuation of the saga of the Calloway family.

Next, many of you eagerly anticipated the next installment of Joan Hohl's BIG BAD WOLFE series—and you don't have to wait any longer. *Wolfe Wanting* is here!

Don't worry if you're starting these series midstream; each book stands alone as a sensuous, compelling romance. So take the plunge.

But there's much more. Four fabulous books you won't want to miss. Kelly Jamison's *The Daddy Factor;* Raye Morgan's *Babies on the Doorstep;* Anne Marie Winston's *Find Her, Keep Her;* and Susan Crosby's *The Mating Game.*

Don't you dare pick and choose! Read them all. If you don't, you'll be missing something wonderful.

All the best,

Lucia Macro
Senior Editor

Please address questions and book requests to:
Silhouette Reader Service
U.S.: 3010 Walden Ave., P.O. Box 1325, Buffalo, NY 14269
Canadian: P.O. Box 609, Fort Erie, Ont. L2A 5X3

ANNETTE BROADRICK

TEMPTATION TEXAS STYLE!

SILHOUETTE *Desire*®
Published by Silhouette Books
America's Publisher of Contemporary Romance

SILHOUETTE BOOKS

ISBN 0-373-05883-7

TEMPTATION TEXAS STYLE!

ANNETTE BROADRICK

believes in romance and the magic of life. Since 1984, when her first book was published, Annette has shared her view of life and love with readers all over the world. In addition to being nominated by *Romantic Times* as one of the Best New Authors of that year, she has also won the *Romantic Times* Reviewer's Choice Award for Best in its Series for *Heat of the Night, Mystery Lover* and *Irresistible;* the *Romantic Times* WISH Award for her heroes in *Strange Enchantment* and *Marriage Texas Style!;* and *Romantic Times* Lifetime Achievement Awards for Series Romance and Series Romantic Fantasy.

One

He should be used to pain by now. Tony shifted gears and grimaced. After all, he'd been part of the rodeo scene since he was fifteen years old...fifteen years ago.

He was a fool for continuing to enter the bullriding events at his age. He was getting too old to punish himself like that, as his body at the moment kept telling him.

He'd left Fort Worth four hours ago. Another hour should see him pulling in at the gate to his place, thank God. He was more than ready to stop the punishment he'd been putting himself through trying to drive. His pickup had a stick shift. Every time he'd had to use the clutch, his left ankle had let him know that he'd done a number on it.

The damn thing was either sprained or broken. He'd probably have to have Clem cut off his boot once he got home.

Rodeoing played hell with his wardrobe as well as his body. Despite all the drawbacks, though, he still loved the excitement, the competition, and the recognition that came with the three belt buckles he'd won that proclaimed him World Champion Bullrider for three years running... which was why he kept putting himself through this punishment.

He lowered the sun visor, adjusted his aviator shades and checked the rearview mirrors to make certain the horse trailer he was pulling was okay. Thank God Clem was at the ranch looking after things. Tony would ask him to unload the cutting horse he'd used for the calf-roping events and put him away while he got his blasted boot off and soaked himself in the tub.

Clem had hired on with him three years ago, the same year Tony had bought his spread with his prize money from following the rodeo circuit. So far they'd managed to get along on the ranch without much outside help. Of course, if Tony's plans to expand his stock worked out, he'd be looking for more help. However, that was somewhere in the future.

For now, Betsy Krueger came out from town once a week to give the house a cleaning, and cooked enough food to freeze so he'd have something to warm up and eat during the week. The rest of the time he rattled around the house by himself.

Tony preferred it that way. He liked living alone, answering to no one. Clem had a room in the barn where he slept, sharing his meals with Tony when he wasn't off to town during the evenings.

Tony liked his life. There were no entanglements, no distractions. If he got lonesome and wanted company, he had a raft of relatives scattered across the state.

He came up over a rise in the road and began to slow down. At the bottom of this long and winding drop was the gate to his place, the T Bar C Ranch.

That gate had never looked so good to him. He wanted to throw himself on a flat surface and not move for a week. Not that he could do that. He had a meeting in town on Monday to discuss his plans for the ranch. He couldn't afford to postpone it. However, he could spend tomorrow—Sunday—lying around with his foot propped up. By the following day he should be feeling all right.

He guided the truck-and-trailer rig into the private lane with his usual skill and followed the road among brush, granite outcrops and occasional cacti to where the ranch house, barn, feed shed and storage garage formed a horseshoe around a circular driveway.

He was already swinging the rig in an arc in front of the barn so that he could park the trailer next to the building when he saw a vehicle he didn't recognize sitting in front of the house.

What the hell? He wasn't expecting anybody. At the moment, company was the last thing he needed or wanted.

He stopped the truck and sat for a moment, staring at the faded red van with the Georgia license plates. He tried to remember if he knew anybody from that part of the country. At the moment, no one came to mind.

"You goin' to sit there all night?" Clem asked, sauntering up to the cab of the truck and peering in at him.

Clem Wilson was tall and as skinny as a rail, his skin weathered from years of working outdoors. Tony had no idea how old Clem was, and he didn't care. He just knew there was very little that Clem didn't know about running a ranch. That was good enough for Tony.

He grabbed his Stetson from beside him, opened the door and gingerly lowered himself to the ground.

"Whadya break this time?" the older man drawled without inflection.

"Nothing! I don't think," Tony replied, wincing when he attempted to put some weight on his left foot.

"Bull step on ya?"

Tony bristled. "Of course not. I just came off a little sloppy and landed wrong."

"Before or after the buzzer?"

Tony grinned. "After, of course."

Clem nudged the brim of his hat with his thumb, turned his head and spit, then rearranged the chewing tobacco in his cheek with his tongue. "It's a wonder ya have any brains left, you've scrambled 'em so many times taking them falls."

Tony nodded toward the house. "Who's at the house?"

Clem shrugged. "Some long-lost relative of your mother's. At least that's what she said."

Tony frowned. "A relative of Mom's? Then what's she doing here?"

"She said the housekeeper at the Austin house told her your mom and dad weren't home and gave her directions to your place."

Tony rubbed his forehead. His headache had grown steadily worse in the hours since he'd finished his bullriding stint. He'd hit the ground pretty hard, and it had jarred him. He was tempted to agree with Clem. His brains must be scrambled by now. What he didn't need at the moment was to have to entertain some visiting biddy, and listen to long, rambling stories of the days when she was just a girl.

"Who is this woman—did she say?"

"Christina O'Reilly."

"Never heard of her."

"She said her great-great-grandmother and your mother's great-grandmother were cousins."

"So? That doesn't make her a real relative of ours, for God's sake."

"Never said it did. She's the one claiming to be your relative."

Dammit! This was the last thing he needed. What rotten timing. She would have to show up the week his folks took the younger kids to Disney World in Florida.

"You want me to put the horse up?"

Damn. He'd been standing here stewing over his unwanted company instead of taking care of chores. "Yeah. I'd appreciate it."

"You'd better get off that ankle. You goin' to need some help getting that boot off?"

"I'm not going to bother saving it. I'll just get a knife and—"

"Let me do it. There's no sense in you—"

"You'll be busy out here. I can do it."

"Don't be so bullheaded, hotshot! Git on inside and prop that leg up. Give me fifteen minutes and I'll be in there to help." Clem spun on his heel and strode to the back of the trailer, muttering to himself. Tony was fairly certain he was meant to overhear a few of the more choice adjectives he used—"stubborn," "arrogant," "simple-minded," and a couple that were bordering on obscene. Nope, not a complimentary comment in the lot.

He hadn't expected to hear one.

He would never have to worry about letting his rodeo fame and accomplishments go to his head, not as long as Clem was around to point out his shortcomings.

Tony started walking toward the house, stifling a groan with every step he took. Damn, but that ankle hurt! Add to that the fact that his entire body was one great big ache, already stiffening up on him. Never had the distance between the barn and the house seemed so long. He'd just—

"Oh, my! You're hurt! Were you in an accident?"

He'd been looking down when he heard the voice coming from the front porch. He glanced up and came to an abrupt halt. What the hell was going on here?

The woman standing by one of the square pillars that supported the porch roof couldn't be over twenty-five years old. Her hair was a riot of corkscrew curls and fiery color, springing around her head and spilling over her bare shoulders.

She wore a skimpy tank top—bright yellow—and a pair of jeans that clung to her slim hips and long legs. Thong sandals were on her feet. Each of her toenails was painted a different color—red, orange, yellow, green and blue.

His gaze returned to her face. Wide-spaced green eyes with a thick fringe of dark lashes stared at him in obvious concern. A sprinkling of freckles decorated her nose.

"*You're* Christina O'Reilly?"

"How did you . . . ? Oh! Mr. Wilson must have told you my name." She danced down the stairs to where he stood staring at her with disbelief and dismay.

"You must be Tony Callaway, Allison's son."

"You know my mother?" His mom had never told him about anyone remotely resembling this person.

Christina gave a quick shake of her head, causing her curls to dance as though they were on springs. "Not yet, but I know a lot about her."

He stiffened. Tony was very protective of his mother and her reputation. If this woman was implying—

"Her mother was Kathleen Brannigan. Kathleen's mother was Moira O'Hara, and Moira's mother was—"

"All right. I don't need a genealogy lesson at the moment, or a recital of my family tree."

The look Christina gave him was tinged with disappointment. "Oh. Genealogy happens to be a hobby of mine. I've been doing it for years. When I decided to visit Texas, I made a list of the names that I had traced to this part of the country. It's fascinating to trace a line, then search to find where that person lives. I've been to Ireland twice and met several people who are distant kin. It's kinda fun since—"

My God, did the woman never shut up? He hobbled past her and grabbed the stair railing, relieved to take some of his weight off his ankle.

"Ohh, you're really hurting, aren't you? What happened?"

He eased up the steps, one at a time. "I landed wrong," he muttered between clenched teeth.

"Landed wrong?" She repeated his words as though they made no sense to her. "You mean you jumped out of something?"

"*Off* of something."

She was moving slowly alongside him as though to encourage him in his efforts. "What did you jump off of?"

He closed his eyes for a moment, wishing he could let out a bellow of pain. When he opened them he saw a pair of worried green eyes watching him.

"A bull," he muttered, making it to the top step and carefully crossing the porch.

"You jumped off a bull?" She sounded incredulous. "How on earth did you happen to be on a bull?"

He opened the screen door and waited impatiently for her to enter. "That's what I do."

She hurried through the door. "You're joking!" She whirled around to face him. "Nobody spends their time jumping off bulls."

"I *ride* them. I'm a bullrider. It's a skill, an art, a..." A slight movement caught his eye and he looked past her shoulder. "What in the hell is that?" He pointed across the living room to the animal stretched out on the braided rug in front of the fireplace.

"It's a dog, of course. I know I should have asked if I could bring him—"

"A dog! Now who's joking? That thing is the size of a horse!"

The object of their discussion raised his massive head and looked at them as though aware he was the topic of discussion. Slowly, he unwound his incredibly long legs and stood on snowshoe-size feet before ambling toward them, his long tail knocking over everything he passed as it waved to and fro in a friendly gesture. His head came to Tony's chest.

"Oh, Hercules! Look what you've done," Christina said with patient exasperation. She rushed over to the table next to the leather couch and scooped up the papers and magazines the dog had knocked to the floor. "He's a Great Dane," she explained, "and he's really very gentle. He wouldn't hurt a soul."

"Unless he sat on them," Tony muttered.

Hercules ducked his head and rubbed his chin against Tony's hand.

"See? He's trying to make friends with you."

"Am I supposed to be flattered?"

Christina straightened and gave him a sparkling smile filled with mischief. The smile caught him unprepared because it totally changed her looks. "I'd like to say yes, but the truth is that Hercules tries to make friends with everybody. That's what's wrong with him."

Tony rubbed the massive head. The tail increased its furious movement. "Wrong?"

She nodded, her smile gone. "His original owners bought him to be trained as a guard dog, but it didn't work out. He was too friendly. Hercules loves everybody. Don't you, precious?" she crooned to the monster.

"So how did you end up with him?"

"They were going to have him put to sleep!" she said indignantly. "I was at the vet's the day his owners brought him in. As soon as I heard what they intended to do, I told them I'd take him myself before I'd let them kill him."

"I see."

The screen door squeaked open and Clem said, "I thought I told you to prop that leg up. Don'cha have a lick o' sense?"

"Here, let me help," Christina said, dashing to his side and wrapping her arm around his waist.

Her unexpected offer startled Tony. "Wha-what do you think you're doing?" he demanded, staring at the woman who was now pressed snugly against his side.

He pushed her away. "I don't need any help, for God's sake."

He wouldn't have needed any help, that is, if Hercules hadn't decided to pursue his newest friendship opportunity by crowding against Tony, causing him to lose his balance. He began to topple, favoring his injured ankle, until Christina grabbed him around the waist again and guided him the few steps to the couch.

Still off-balance, they both fell, luckily landing on the couch with Tony on his back and Christina sprawled across him.

She didn't weigh much. That was his first thought as he measured her length against his. Her small breasts were pressed against his chest, and from this angle he could see down the front of her tank top, confirming what he'd already noticed the moment he saw her—she wasn't wearing a bra.

One of his thighs was between her legs, and as she squirmed against him, he was acutely aware of other intimate parts of her anatomy.

"Oh! I'm so sorry," she said, wriggling away from him. "Hercules! Leave his hat alone. That's no way to make friends with people."

By the time she'd managed to push away from him and get up, Tony felt that a permanent impression of her body had been stamped upon his.

"You okay, Boss?" Clem asked from somewhere behind the couch. Tony could almost hear the snicker in his voice.

He considered himself a mature male with a fair degree of patience, but he wasn't a saint, dammit, which was what any person would have to be to tolerate Ms. Christina O'Reilly and her horse named Hercules.

"Of course I'm not okay," he bellowed, stretched out flat on his back and feeling like a complete fool. He struggled to push himself up onto his elbows.

He glared at Christina, then turned to annihilate Clem with another glare just as a blur of yellow fur flew past his face and landed on his chest.

"Wha' the—?"

"Oh, Prometheus, not now! I don't think Mr. Callaway is ready to meet you just yet."

A pair of slanted topaz eyes stared unblinkingly at Tony a few inches from his nose. Ears lay flat against a broad, round head. The cat was a solid weight on his chest.

"Prometheus?" he repeated incredulously.

"Well, he wasn't exactly chained to a rock, but he was caught in a horrible trap. He almost died! The vet couldn't save his foot, but he's gotten along just fine without it." Christina leaned over Tony, either unaware or unconcerned that he was given another view of her chest clear to her belly button, and scooped up the short-haired, tiger-striped cat.

Only then did Tony see that the animal was missing a front paw.

"Don't tell me, let me guess. They were going to have him put to sleep and you—"

"Oh, no! I was the one who found him. It was when I was practicing for a marathon. I'd found a route I liked in the country and was following a series of farm roads. I heard him late one afternoon as I was making one of my laps. It was awful. I didn't know how to help him and he was in so much pain. I ran to the closest farmhouse. The farmer helped me by finding a grain sack and putting the cat and the trap inside. He swore that it wasn't his trap. Anyway, I drove Pro-

metheus to the vet's office. The man had to put him to
sleep before he could get the trap off his leg. He did
everything he could, but there was no way he could
save the paw."

"You and the vet must be buddies by now," he said
sarcastically, but she took his comment at face value.
"Yes, we are. I once thought I wanted to be a veteri-
narian but discovered I couldn't handle seeing the animals in pain. I couldn't even work in the office,
although I've filled in on a few emergencies when his
regular help was unable to come in. Filling in like that
proved to me I'd made the right decision. I just
couldn't be that detached when I knew what they were
going through."

"Uh, Boss?"

"Yes, Clem?" Tony answered wearily, this time
managing to sit up.

"About your ankle...?"

"Yeah, I know. Get a knife from the kitchen."

"A knife!" Christina echoed, horrified. "You can't
mean to—" She glanced down at the cat in her arms
and hugged him to her before she stared at Tony's
booted foot.

"Oh, for crying out loud," he muttered, looking
over his shoulder to make certain Clem was headed
toward the kitchen. That's when he saw Hercules
pawing at his black Stetson, which he'd placed on the
nearby table.

"Hey! Get away from there!"

His sudden bellow startled the dog, the cat and the
woman. The dog backed up, bumping into the floor
lamp and causing it to swing alarmingly; the cat leaped
to the back of an armchair nearby and hissed, the fur

on his perpendicular tail standing on end; the woman gave a startled yelp.

"'Deliver me, O Lord, from the evil man and preserve me from the violent man,'" a hoarse, sepulchral voice intoned.

Clem came striding into the room, waving a lethal-looking butcher knife. "What in blue thunder was that?"

Christina clasped her hands and held them rigidly at her waist. "I can explain. I'm really sorry. She's usually very quiet. I mean, most of the time I forget she's around."

"Who are you talking about?" Tony demanded, looking around the room for some demented female.

"Minerva."

"Who in blazes is Minerva?" he shouted.

"'Keep me, O Lord, from the hands of the wicked.'"

"I think your shouting upsets her," Christina said quietly.

Tony counted very slowly to ten and decided to keep going. By the time he reached twenty-five, he believed he could trust himself to speak once more.

"Who..." There. He sounded calm "...is Minerva?"

"Clara Bledsoe's mynah bird."

He nodded as though her answer made perfect sense to him. "I see. And who is Clara Bledsoe?"

"My next-door neighbor. Or at least she was. She's the sweetest thing. Eighty-two years young and a joy to know. Full of sprightly fun and energy. Truly a delightful person." She paused for breath, brushing a cluster of corkscrew curls behind her ear. "She broke her hip a few weeks ago and had to move into a nursing home. It was so sad. She had to sell or give away most everything she had accumulated over the years. She has no family. She said I was just like a daughter to her.''

This woman was out of her cotton-pickin' mind. Why hadn't he understood that immediately? Shouldn't the multicolored toenails have told him something?

He was determined to humor her in hopes of getting her out of here as soon as possible. ''So...because she thought of you as a daughter,'' he continued her story helpfully, ''she gave you her bird?''

''I guess. I mean, they wouldn't let her have Minerva in the nursing home and there was really no one else, you see.''

''Oh, absolutely.'' He shifted on the couch and motioned for Clem to come over. ''So, tell me, Ms. O'Reilly. What other surprises do you have for us this evening? A blind Bengal tiger lurking in the van? A deaf rhinoceros, perhaps? I'd rather have some kind of warning, if you don't mind.'' He was being as pleasant as he knew how to be, given his circumstances.

''There aren't any more,'' she said quickly. ''Honestly. Usually none of them are any trouble at all. The thing is, Mrs. Bledsoe taught Minerva several Bible verses and sometimes when she's disturbed, she starts quoting them.''

''What, exactly—besides loud voices, of course— seems to upset Minerva?'' Tony asked, looking around the room in an effort to spot the Bible-spouting bird. Once alerted to the presence of another visitor, he had no problem locating her. The cage was sitting in one of the corners by a window, and it held a black bird crouched on a perch, balefully eyeing him.

"That's all, really. Sometimes, when she's in a particularly philosophical mood, she'll offer food for thought, but on the whole, she doesn't say much."

"Thank the Lord," he muttered.

"Amen," Minerva added with solemn dignity.

"C'mon, Clem. Get this boot off."

Clem knelt beside the couch and looked at the expensive boot leather. "Are you sure you don't want to try to pull it off?"

"It won't come off. Not now. Just do it."

Christina hurried around the couch and leaned over the back to watch as Clem carefully worked the sharp point of the knife into the leather. The movement caused stabbing pains all around the ankle. Tony caught his breath and clenched his jaw.

"Am I hurtin' ya?" Clem asked.

"Just get it off, will you?"

"Here," Christina said, holding out her hand to him. "Squeeze my hand when the pain gets too intense."

He stared at her slim hand as though it were a poisonous snake. If Clem dared to laugh, so help him, he'd deck him.

"Thank you," he replied, "but if it gets too bad, I have some bullets in my pocket I can chew on."

He ignored Clem's throat clearing.

She looked stunned, as well she should. "Really? You mean people really do bite bullets?"

"Only in Texas. You ever been here before?" he asked, trying to ignore the excruciating pain as Clem continued to work on the boot.

"No. This is my first visit."

"We're a different breed of people down here, you know," he confided. "Like no place you've ever been."

She eyed him uncertainly. "In what way?"

"Well, we're not really civilized. Of course, we know how to pretend around other folks when we have to, but most of the time we just enjoy our primitive pleasures."

"There!" Clem said with satisfaction. "Lordy, boy, but you did it up good this time."

Tony looked down and watched as his discolored foot, now free of both boot and sock, swelled before their eyes. No longer restrained by the boot, the blood rushed into the injured area with an insistent throb that made his head swim.

"Shouldn't you get some ice on that?" Christina asked.

Her voice was fading in and out as the room began to spin.

"Good idee," Clem replied, standing. "I'll make him up an ice pack and see if we can get that swelling under control."

The room darkened and shimmered around him. The last thing Tony heard before he passed out was Minerva's eerie voice hoarsely offering her philosophical comment on the moment, "'I will not leave you comfortless.'"

Two

"Mother," Tony said into the phone early the next morning while he was still in bed. "I know you've been promising Katie and the boys this trip for the past two years, but you've got to come home!"

Allison Callaway sounded much too young to have a thirty-year-old son. She also looked too young. People who met her for the first time had trouble believing that she was the mother of a fourteen-year-old daughter and eleven-year-old twin sons.

Young or not, she definitely sounded like a worried parent. "Oh, no, Tony! What happened? How bad is it? Are you in the hospital? Where—?"

"Whoa, whoa, Mom, calm down. I'm not hurt. Well, I sprained my ankle, but that's nothing," he said, dismissing his wimpish fainting spell of the evening before. He'd forgotten to eat lunch yesterday, that's all. His blood sugar had dropped too low and fainting had been the perfectly natural result.

"Then what is it?"

"You've got a visitor."

"Tony Callaway, what are you talking about? You aren't making any sense whatsoever."

Patiently, he attempted to explain. "There's a woman here who came to Texas to meet family members she's found on her genealogy chart. She says that one of her long-gone ancestors was a cousin of one of your long-gone ancestors, and she seems to think you'd be delighted to make her acquaintance."

"Well, maybe I would. What's her name?"

"Christina O'Reilly. She says she's been living in Atlanta for the past five years."

"I don't know of any relations in Atlanta."

"Well, if you have any, she'll know everything about them, believe me."

"Who are her parents?"

"Hell, I don't remember all the names. She rattled off so many last night my head was swimming." Which was the God's truth.

"Tony, watch your language."

"Yes'm. Anyway, she said her folks were killed when she was four and that she was raised in an orphanage. Maybe that's why she's so interested in her bloodlines. Who knows? The thing is, Mom, she's weird."

"What do you mean, weird?"

"Strange...loony...bonkers. She's traveling with a dog the size of a horse that she calls Hercules, a three-legged cat she named Prometheus—don't ask me to try to explain that one. I was never interested in

Greek mythology—and a Bible-verse-spouting my-nah bird named Minerva.''

Tony stared stonily out the window and waited while his mother laughed her fool head off. When she began to run down, he said, "I'm real pleased to know you find all of this so blasted amusing. Why don't you do me this big favor...come on home so *you* can entertain Christina and her zoo and get 'em out of my hair."

"She's there with you now?"

"Oh yeah. She went to your place first and Carlita gave her directions here."

"Good for Carlita. I'm looking forward to meeting this Christina. She sounds like a wonderful person to me."

"Glad *you* think so," he muttered. "Then you'll come home right away?"

"Next weekend," she corrected gently. "We should land in Austin around noon next Sunday."

"But that's a whole week!"

"So?"

"So what am I supposed to do with this woman for a week?"

"Entertain her?" she suggested helpfully.

"How do you propose I do that? I'm laid up with this ankle. Clem's having to take care of the stock for me until I can get a boot back on."

"Have you talked to the bank about your loan?"

"I have an appointment in the morning."

"You know that your dad and I would be—"

"Mom, we've already discussed it. The answer's no. I'm doing this on my own or not at all...remember?"

"Oh, you're so stubborn! There are times I get terribly frustrated trying to deal with you."

"I come by it honestly, and you know it."

"Not true. At least I'm open to discussion and can be reasonable."

"I was referring to Dad."

She laughed. "Point taken. As for Christina, I don't see why you can't have a little compassion for her. After all, you grew up without a father. It seems to me you might be able to understand how she felt growing up without either parent."

Good ol' Mom. She zeroed straight in to the guilt button. He didn't know how she managed to nail it every time with unerring precision.

"Next Sunday, you said?" he asked wearily, conceding defeat.

"Yes."

He gave a big sigh. "All right, but remember, you owe me big time for this one. I don't know exactly what it'll be, but I'll think of something."

"Really, Tony, how hard can entertaining be? She's probably a warm and tenderhearted person. How old is she?"

"I didn't ask. I guess somewhere in her twenties."

"Good-looking?"

"I don't know."

"Take your blinders off, Son. There's a whole wide world out there besides ranches and rodeos."

"Don't start. If you're implying that I should become interested in this retro hippy, you're—"

"Do you have any idea how stuffy you sound? Sometimes it's hard for me to believe that you're actually my flesh and blood."

He grinned, thinking about his mother's artistic temperament, her use of bright colors and some of her more outlandish choices of clothing. "Maybe I took after Dad more than I realized. Come to think about it, you and Christina *do* seem to have a lot in common."

"Is she a sculptor, too?"

"I haven't asked. But if she's going to be here an entire week, I'll probably know everything there is to know about her by the time you arrive," he said, rubbing the bridge of his nose wearily.

"You'll do just fine, I'm sure," she said reassuringly. "Do you want to say hello to your dad?"

"Not now. I've got to get going. Tell him hi, give the kids a hug for me. I'll see y'all Sunday."

He hung up before Allison could ignore his response and hand the phone to Cole. He knew that sooner or later he and his dad were going to have to talk, but Tony wasn't ready. In the meantime, he avoided one-on-one conversations with him as much as possible, shielding himself with the noise and boisterous confusion that occurred whenever the rest of the family was around as well.

He glanced at his watch. He should have been up an hour ago. Whatever it was Clem had given him last evening had done the trick. He'd slept through the night without stirring, which was probably why he felt much better this morning. The ankle twinged a little when he flexed it, but with the swelling down, the pain had subsided.

He tossed the covers back and got out of bed, intending to shower and dress. With his first step, however, his foot hit an obstruction lying by the bed. With a yelp of surprise and helpless indignation, Tony landed with a resounding thud on the thick carpet.

Hercules let out his own yelp of surprise and lumbered to his feet, towering over Tony, who rolled to his back and lay reciting the dog's lineage at some length.

Hercules gave him an enthusiastic swipe with his ten-foot tongue to show his appreciation of the attention.

The bedroom door flew open.

"What happened? Are you all right?" Christina rushed in and stared, horrified, at the two of them.

Tony was not dressed for company. He was bare except for a pair of black bikini briefs. He glared at the woman, whose eyes had grown to an enormous size since the last time he'd seen her. He pulled himself off the floor by grabbing one of the bedposts and asked, "What in the hell is that dog doing in my room?"

She wrung her hands. "He wanted to stay close to you. He was worried about you."

"He told you that?"

"He didn't have to. His actions were quite plain."

In a lower voice, he asked, "How did he get in here without my knowing it?"

She offered him a tentative smile. "You must have fallen asleep within minutes after Clem helped you to bed last night. He'd just left when I heard Hercules scratching at your door. I opened it to see if you'd mind if he came in. You were sound asleep. Hercules took advantage of the open door and immediately rushed in. After sniffing your hand and nosing your cheek, he collapsed beside the bed, put his head on his paws and closed his eyes." She gave a little shrug. "He's impossible to move if he doesn't want to go, so I ended up leaving him in here. I'm truly sorry if he disturbed you."

This morning she was wearing a dress...of sorts. At least there was a skirt. It was a rainbow of swirling colors that hung to her ankles. However, it was so thin that he could see through it. She was wearing some kind of leggings underneath. The top was of the same material but doubled or something, because he couldn't see through it. Thin shoulder straps held the top up. He had a hunch she'd dispensed with a bra today as well.

He wondered if she even owned one.

With as much dignity as possible given the present circumstances, Tony sat down on the side of the bed and jerked the covers over his lap. "I talked to my mother this morning," he said politely, "and told her you were here. She's delighted you've come to visit."

Christina's face lit up. "Oh, I'm so glad. I'm looking forward to meeting her. Did she say when she'd be home?"

"Sunday."

Her face fell. "Next Sunday?" she repeated, sounding dismayed. "But that's a week away."

"I know."

She looked around the room with a sense of uncertainty and concern. "But I can't stay here for a week."

"Why not?"

"Because I don't want to take advantage of your hospitality that way."

He rubbed the back of his neck for a moment before asking, "Can you cook?"

Her brows drew together. Puzzled, she replied, "Certainly."

"Then you won't need to worry that you might be taking advantage. You can cook for us."

"Us?"

"Me and Clem."

She thought about his offer. After a lengthy silence, she slowly said, "I suppose I could."

"Then it's settled." Tony shifted slightly and concentrated on meticulously rearranging the covers across his lap.

"I thought you were upset with my animals," she said after another long silence. She watched him carefully, her hands hidden in the folds of her filmy skirt.

Couldn't put anything past this woman, he thought dryly.

"I'm sure I'll adjust all right once I get used to them," he said, mentally reviewing what he was going to extract from his mother in payment for a week of being a zookeeper.

Christina suddenly broke into one of her brilliant smiles, which seemed to catch him off guard every time he saw one. He thought about what his mother had asked. *All right,* he admitted to himself, *I guess she's good-looking, in a bohemian kind of way.*

Straightening to her full height and facing him unflinchingly, she said, "I took it upon myself to make you breakfast. I hope you don't mind."

Now here was some good news. He'd always relied on his own cooking for breakfast and he wasn't the most inspired chef around. He smiled at her, determined to show her he could be friendly. "That sounds great. I'm starved." He waited for her to leave.

Instead, she asked, "Would you like me to bring it to you?"

What was the matter with her? Did she think he was some kind of invalid? "No!" She flinched and he tried to modify his response by lowering his voice a little. "But, uh, thanks for offering. I'll come get it as soon as I'm *dressed.*" He stressed the last word and had the pleasure of seeing her cheeks turn red.

Had it just now occurred to her that she was in his bedroom and that he was practically nude?

She spun away. Without looking at him she said, "The biscuits should be ready in about five minutes." She stepped back into the hall and jerked the door closed behind her.

He looked at Hercules, who'd been sitting on his haunches observing the conversation like a spectator at a tennis match. Now that they were alone, the dog rose in a welter of legs and ambled over to the bed. He rested his chin on Tony's knee with a sigh, rolling his eyes.

"Biscuits?" Tony repeated to himself thoughtfully, absently stroking the dog's head. "She can make biscuits? This may not be such a bad trade-off after all."

He gently pushed the dog aside and stood, this time making it to the bathroom without mishap.

Although the day hadn't started well for Tony's sense of order and comforting routine, he had to admit that maybe things weren't going to be as bad as he'd thought.

Christina hurried down the hall, appalled by her behavior and embarrassed that she'd made such a complete fool of herself. How could she have barged into the man's room without so much as a knock?

The shock of finding him on the floor had been almost as great as seeing him undressed.

She hadn't needed a reminder of how strongly she was drawn to Tony Callaway.

From the time she saw him yesterday, Christina had known that Tony was different from any man she'd ever known. She'd been fascinated by his tall, lean body with its wide, muscled shoulders, slim hips and long muscular legs. He'd moved with athletic grace across the ranch yard despite the hesitation before he placed his weight on his injured ankle.

He had a hard look about him, as though he didn't find much in life to laugh about, and a fierce toughness that had been apparent in his attitude toward his injury.

His black Stetson had shielded his face from her view until he'd gotten close to the house. He'd looked up when she'd spoken and her breath had caught.

He had a face that could have been used as a model for Michael, the militant archangel. It had a purity of sculpted lines and planes—a wide forehead, deep-set black eyes, high cheekbones, a strong jawline and a mouth that tempted her with its sensuous curve.

The shock of seeing such male beauty had shaken her, and in her nervousness she'd rattled on like a complete idiot, making an awful hash of their meeting.

She checked the biscuits and quickly placed them on top of the stove, then went back to mixing eggs for the omelets she was preparing. A stack of finely chopped vegetables, ham and cheese waited to be included in the dish.

It would be a long time before she forgot her reaction when she'd returned to the living room with Clem last night and discovered Tony had fainted.

Hercules had been by his side, nudging him, a soft whimpering sound coming from the dog's throat.

"Blast him anyway," Clem muttered, wrapping the bag of ice around Tony's ankle. "He's gotta be so all-fired macho about his injuries. I knew that pain was gettin' to him, but no, he ain't goin' to admit it to no-body.''

She knelt beside Tony, fighting the desire to brush his hair off his forehead. Without the scowl, he looked even more like her image of a sword-wielding angel, his brow gleaming with a faint sheen of moisture, his features at peace.

"Is he going to be all right?" she whispered.

"Not from any smart thinkin' on his part. I can't remember the number of bones he's broke riding in those rodeo competitions. Ribs, arms and legs...once he punctured a lung. To him a sprain ain't nothing.'' He shook his head in disgust.

"Should we try to bring him to?"

"No way. He needs the rest! 'Sides, he's gettin' some relief from the pain. He drove all the way from Fort Worth with this thing hurtin'. Most people would have had the smarts to get a room for a day or two and rest, maybe get the thing x-rayed and wrapped. But this guy don't have a lick o' sense.''

"You admire him a lot, don't you?" she asked softly.

Clem's eyes cut toward her and he gave her a fero-cious frown. "Admire him? When he don't take care of hisself? Huh! But I knowed him since he was in di-apers. Watched him growing up without a daddy. His mama did a fine job of raising the boy. Sure can't blame her for his stubbornness.''

"But I thought Cole Callaway was his father," she said, puzzled. According to her research, Cole and Allison had four children—Tony, Katie, Clint and Cade.

"He is. There's no doubt in anybody's mind that Tony's a Callaway...looks like 'em, acts like 'em." He shook his head ruefully.

"I don't understand. Where was his dad when Tony was growing up?"

"Playing Mr. Big Shot Callaway of the Texas Callaways, busy running the family's businesses. The family must own a hunk o' Texas. Can't pick up a paper or watch TV that they aren't in the news doing somethin' or another."

"He ignored his wife and son?"

Clem seemed to realize that he was gossiping about his employer and that Tony would have his neck if he found out. He glanced uneasily at the man who still lay relaxed in front of them and cleared his throat.

"To give the fella his due, he didn't find out that Tony even existed until the boy was almost fifteen. He was practically growed up by then. Ol' Cole did what he could, I'll give 'im that. He married Allison, moved her and Tony to Austin, put Tony through college, but Tony had already developed his independent ways. He still goes his own way pretty much, regardless of what the family might want for him."

"What do they want him to do?"

Clem shrugged. "Dunno. Maybe spend more time with 'em, maybe get involved in the family businesses. Tony's uncle, Cameron, works closely with Cole. Tony is more like his maverick uncle, Cody, who's busy raising horses on the family ranch south of San Antonio. Don't want no truck with the business world. Tony's the same way."

Unable to resist the temptation any longer, Christina lightly brushed Tony's hair back from his forehead. His eyelids quivered and he groaned.

"I think he's coming to," she whispered.

Clem nodded. "Good thing, I guess. He'll still be in a heap o' pain, but I think he's got some pain pills left over from the last time he got banged around. I'll get some and see if we can get a couple down him while he's too groggy to protest."

Christina had been alone with Tony—if she ignored the presence of a curious dog, a haughty cat and a sleeping bird—when he opened his eyes. He blinked at her as though he didn't believe what he was seeing.

"Hi," she said softly. "Remember me?"

He closed his eyes for a moment before opening them again. He looked at the room in confusion. "What happened? Did I fall asleep?"

She nibbled on her bottom lip to keep from smiling. "You're probably tired after your long trip today," she replied.

Before Tony could respond, Clem strode back into the room carrying a glass of water and a capsule. "Here. Take this," he said, thrusting them both at Tony.

Tony pushed himself into a sitting position, wincing when he moved his foot. "What is it?"

"Don't matter. Take it." He continued to hold out the items.

Tony reached for them slowly.

"When's the last time you ate?" Clem asked.

"Breakfast, I think."

"Well, hell, man. How do you expect to keep going without fuel? I'll heat ya up some of that stew." He turned and left the room.

Christina watched Tony look blankly at the capsule he was holding. She held her breath, waiting to see what he would do, then released it when he rolled his shoulders in a shrug and swallowed the medication.

"Guess I was tireder than I thought," he muttered, not meeting her eyes.

Only then did she realize that she was still kneeling beside him as he sat on the couch. She quickly stood and turned away.

Minerva caught her eye. Thankful for something to do, she went over and placed the colorful cloth cover Mrs. Bledsoe had made around the birdcage. When she turned back, Tony was watching her.

"The guest bedroom's at the end of the hall," he said, nodding in that direction. "I'll have Clem carry your bags in."

"I didn't intend to stay this long," she explained a little nervously. "I thought you could tell me when your mother would be home and I'd be on my way."

"It's too late for you to go anywhere tonight. We can talk more tomorrow." He pushed himself off the couch just as Clem brought in a tray with a bowl of savory stew. "I'll eat that in my room," he told him. "Why don't you help Christina with her things and see that she has something to eat, okay? I think I'm going to turn in. It's been a long day."

Christina had found the bowl half-empty when she'd followed Hercules into his room later.

She heard Tony's bedroom door open and hurriedly slid his omelet onto a warm plate, setting it on the table. She was pouring coffee when he appeared in the doorway.

He'd showered and shaved and looked incredibly appealing to her in a blue chambray shirt that stretched snugly across his wide chest, and a pair of jeans that were faded almost white from repeated washings. He'd put on a pair of moccasins that no doubt provided him with a little more comfort than his boots.

"Smells great," he said, flashing a quick grin at her. "You're definitely worth keeping around for a while."

She knew he was teasing her, knew he was trying to reassure her, but her silly heart raced at his words, anyway.

Of course he didn't mean it. Now that he was feeling a little better, he was putting himself out to be more charming. She had a hunch this man could charm anything he wanted from a person, male or female. For a flash, Christina wondered how it would feel to have a man as charismatic as Tony Callaway want her. Then reality came into focus and she reminded herself that her childhood had been left behind years ago. She'd learned not to waste her energy on fairy-tale wishes and fanciful dreams.

A man like Tony Callaway would never become a permanent part of her life.

Three

"**D**oes Clem have breakfast with you?" she asked, ready to serve the second omelet.

Tony hadn't said much since sitting down to breakfast, but he'd shown his appreciation for her efforts by steadily eating his way through the plate-size omelet and half a pan of biscuits.

"Sometimes, but not this morning. He takes off early on Sundays and spends the day with friends. Sometimes he visits his brother over in Bandera. I won't see him until tomorrow morning."

"Oh." She looked at the omelet, then put it on another plate and sat down across from him. "Would you help me eat this?" she asked. "I could eat maybe half of it. I thought Clem would be here."

He looked at her plate, then at her. "You sure you can't eat it all?"

She grinned at the eager expression on his face and handed him the plate. "Positive."

He carefully cut the omelet in half and gave the plate back to her. She took a bite. Umm. It *was* good, particularly after the time it had taken to prepare it. She ate until she was full before returning her attention to the man seated across from her.

"What do you do on Sundays when you don't have uninvited company drop in on you?"

He grinned. "Uninvited, maybe, but definitely not unwanted. You certainly know your way around a kitchen, lady. You cook like a professional."

"Actually, I *have* cooked for a living. I've done alot of things to make a living."

He leaned back in his chair, tilting it back on two legs and sipping his coffee. "Yeah? Like what?"

She did a quick mental review of her life before saying, "I left Birmingham as soon as I graduated from high school. I'd just turned seventeen."

"That's a little young to graduate, isn't it?"

"I skipped the third grade."

"Ah. Go ahead."

"I went to Nashville and started busing tables until I graduated to waitressing. I made pretty good money at that, but one night one of the kitchen help got sick and they asked me to fill in. I found I liked working in the kitchen, creating things. It was a nice change from waiting tables, even if it didn't pay as well."

"How long did you do that?"

"Until I saved up the money for business school."

"Good for you. So you went back to school and . . . ?"

"Learned about computers and accounting and took some other business courses, got a two-year certificate and hired out as a temp."

"A temp?"

"A temporary employee. You know, where businesses call to have someone fill in for vacation and sick leave of permanent employees."

"Why didn't you find a permanent position yourself?"

"Because I wasn't sure what I wanted to do. I decided to learn as many skills as possible and try as many different jobs as I could qualify for before settling down somewhere. Once I could afford transportation, I was no longer stuck in one place. That's when I started following my dream."

Tony leaned forward, watching her with interest. "Tell me about your dream."

She realized that she'd been talking to this man as though she'd known him for years. It was true she was naturally outgoing, but because of her interest in people, she was usually the one to draw *them* out.

A sudden shyness swept over her and she looked down at her empty plate. "It sounds silly, really."

"So what? If it's your dream, why do you care how it sounds to others?"

Her gaze flew to his. He still had his dark eyes focused on her, with a slight smile curving that sensuous mouth.

Oh, my. Nobody should look that good this early in the day.

She'd already blabbed this long, so she might as well go on, she decided. And he really did appear to be interested. She played with her water glass without looking at him before saying, "I really didn't mind living in an orphanage. It could have been so much worse after my parents died. The authorities looked for relatives, but both my mother and father were only children of only children.''

"My mom was an only child, too, but she made up for it this generation," he said.

That's when she remembered what Clem had told her about Tony and how he'd grown up. Maybe he *would* understand a little of what she'd felt as a child.

"I was treated very well and I received a good education. There were a couple of times when there was talk about my being adopted, but nothing ever came of it. The thing is, we were always closely supervised everywhere we went. Everything had to be planned out well in advance. We were taken on outings on a regular basis, but nothing was done spontaneously or impulsively... and we never went much farther than the surrounding countryside." She could still remember her frustration with the careful routine of her daily life. "I used to dream about someday being old enough to be able to be on my own, where I didn't have to meet a planned schedule, live an orderly life, dress a certain way, behave in a prescribed manner. I wanted to be free to roam whenever I decided to leave a place." She smiled at him. "I wanted to enjoy my primitive pleasures, as you called them last night, without having to pretend to be civilized."

"I was having a little fun with you last night," he admitted sheepishly.

"Maybe, but I think there're a lot of us in this world who feel just as you said—we only pretend to be civilized when we have to be. I admired you for being so honest about it."

Hercules ambled in from the hallway and headed for the door to the porch. Christina jumped up from her chair. "You've got to go outside, don't you, precious?" she said, opening the door for him.

The dog glanced around at Tony for a long moment, then walked past her.

"What was that look for?" Tony asked.

"Making sure you're all right."

"He's a regular Florence Nightingale." He picked up his plate and cup and headed toward the sink.

"Oh, leave those. I'll get them," she said, returning to the table for her dishes.

"No way. If you cook, I wash up. That's the rule in this house."

She looked at him, surprised. "Really?"

"Well, actually, since I live alone, I generally do both, but I cheat on the cooking part. A friend comes out from town every week to clean for me. She prepares several dishes and puts them in the freezer, so all I have to do is heat them up. I'm not going to know how to act, being able to eat some freshly cooked meals around here."

Christina set her dishes on the counter next to the sink, which Tony was already filling with soapy water.

"Have you always lived on a ranch?" she asked, wanting to change the subject.

"Nope. I lived in town until the middle of my fifteenth year. I spent my summers after that on the family ranch, but the rest of the time I went to school in Austin."

"How long have you had this place?"

"About three years. I want to start raising and training rodeo livestock. I've always been fascinated with rodeo skills. Over the years I've learned what they look for to stock the shows." He gave her a lopsided smile as he glanced at her. "I'm obviously getting too old to be out there myself much longer."

"You said you were riding a bull yesterday?" She wiped down the stove and counter while he was working at the sink. "Are they wild bulls?"

"Supposed to be—the meaner the better."

"How do you know if you're doing it right...if you stay on?"

"Partly. At the very least, you have to stay on the bull's back for eight seconds, which can be the longest eight seconds in a person's life, let me tell you. But there are other rules. You've got to keep one hand high over your head so the judge can see you're holding on with only one hand. You've got to work those spurs to make sure you get the best ride and, of course, you've got to keep from getting yourself killed. Sometimes it's the luck of the draw. Some bulls make you look better than others."

"So you're competing against time and not the other contestants?"

"Yeah. I mean, we compete, but everybody involved with the rodeo is a buddy. It's the cowboy against the animal, not each other."

"So when you go to the rodeo, that's what you do—ride bulls?"

"That's what I really work on during the season, to build points. Occasionally, if the rodeo's near enough that I can take my own horse, I do team roping."

She leaned against the counter, watching him. "Fascinating. I had no idea about any of this."

"You've never seen a rodeo?"

She shook her head.

"If you hang around for a while, I'll take you to one."

A sudden rush of giddiness made her want to shout and throw her arms around his neck with glee, but she reminded herself that she had to at least act like an adult. "I'd like that," she said softly.

There was a scratching at the door and she went to let in Hercules. When she turned back to Tony, he was at the door to the hallway.

"I'm ready to get off this ankle for a while. Let's go into the living room."

Hercules bounded past her and disappeared around the corner, following his newfound friend. She knew exactly how the dog felt. Oh, to be able to express her feelings so freely.

The tantalizing aroma of Tony's after-shave still clung to the kitchen. She followed it into the other room.

Tony was amazed to discover that he was actually enjoying himself. Christina was different from other women he'd met. She didn't do any of the things that the women he knew did to gain his attention.

She didn't stutter and stammer around him, blushing and giggling every time she said something to him.

She didn't flutter her eyelashes and give him seductive looks from the corner of her eyes.

She didn't give him soft little pats or accidentally brush against him.

In short, she didn't flirt with him at all. She looked him in the eye when she spoke to him. She did nothing to indicate that she was attracted to him.

He sank down into his easy chair and propped his foot up on the stool. Hercules sank down beside him with a loud sigh and closed his eyes. Tony watched Christina enter the room and sit on the couch across from him.

"You mentioned last night that you'd lived in Atlanta for five years. You must like it there."

She slipped off her shoes and tucked her feet beneath her before answering him. "Actually, I thought I'd found a career there, but as it turned out, I was wrong." She sounded sad.

"What happened?"

"I took a temporary job in the accounting department at one of the large banks in Atlanta. I really enjoyed that job and decided to apply for a permanent position when one opened." She sighed. "I thought I was doing okay. I mean, I got a couple of raises, I set up some new systems and streamlined the reporting techniques. I felt like I finally had a handle on my life and career." She fiddled with one of her bracelets. "Then they fired me," she said in a low voice.

He straightened. "Fired you! Why?" He felt almost as incensed as she must have been.

"The reasons they gave didn't make much sense. I suppose I could have fought the dismissal, but what good would that have done? I decided that I didn't want to be there if they didn't want me." She rested her head on the back of the couch and looked at him, her smile wistful. "That's when I decided to visit Texas. Who knows? If I like it, maybe I'll look for a job here."

"You're quite a woman, Christina O'Reilly."

"Not really."

"I'd say you're definitely one of a kind. I would like to know, though—why are your toenails each a different color?"

She blinked once, obviously not expecting the abrupt change of subject. "My toes? Oh. I did that to remind myself about the rainbow." She straightened one of her legs and looked at her foot. "The rainbow is a reminder that we should never give up hope. Whenever I forget to look ahead, and look down instead, I remember that I need to keep on with my journey, no matter what happens."

" 'Let not your heart be troubled,' " the voice of a kindly old woman said.

Tony jumped and Christina chuckled. "Sorry. That's Minerva doing Mrs. Bledsoe. She's really amazing. She can sound like anyone. I've had to be very careful not to allow her to listen to television. She picks up remarks very quickly."

" 'Ye are the salt of the earth.' "

"So what's got her started this morning?"

"Who knows? Maybe she just wants to be part of the conversation."

He looked around the room. "I haven't seen your cat this morning."

"He's asleep on my bed. He had a busy night, checking the house out for scurrilous creatures. He dragged himself in and threw himself at my feet this morning, convinced that he now has the place properly secured against all invaders."

"Your animals have been company for you, haven't they?"

She nodded. "I had to move out of my apartment and rent a small house when Hercules joined us. He's only been with me a few months. I found Prometheus three years ago."

"And Minerva?"

"I've known her since I first moved to Atlanta and lived next door to Mrs. Bledsoe, but I've only had her a few weeks. Whenever I can, I take Mrs. Bledsoe out for lunch, then home to visit with Minerva. I know they miss each other. I'm gone for a large part of the day. I hate to make judgments, but I think Minerva sulks."

Tony tried not to laugh. "Really?"

"I know she talks much more around Mrs. Bledsoe than she does around me. That's why she's surprised me here." She cocked her head speculatively. "She must like you. I bet children and animals love you, don't they?"

He thought of his brothers and sister, the horde of cousins, and said, "I guess. I never thought about it."

She was quiet for several moments before she said, "Is my staying here with you going to cause you any trouble?"

"Trouble? What kind of trouble?"

"You said you live alone, so I know you aren't married. I figured you must be seeing someone and that she might not understand my being here."

"I'm not *seeing* anyone, as you so delicately put it, but even if I were, there's no reason why you can't stay here."

"Oh, I know I'm not the sort of person who causes jealousy, but if she only heard about me, she might—"

"Whoa, wait a minute. What do you mean, you're not the sort of person to cause jealousy? Explain that remark."

Her cheeks pinkened. "I shouldn't have to. It's obvious."

"Not to me."

"I'm nobody's idea of a femme fatale," she muttered, obviously embarrassed.

"So? Why would you want to be? You're a very attractive, intelligent, original-thinking woman who needs to make no apologies to anyone about anything."

Her face had now turned a bright red. "Oh, please. I'm sorry. I wasn't trying to get you to pay me any compliments. That's beyond the call of duty of a conscientious host."

He sat up in his chair and stared at her. She was serious. She thought he'd made up everything he'd just said to make her feel better. The shock of it all was that until he started listing what he'd noticed about her, he hadn't realized just how true his comments were. She *was* intelligent and damned attractive. It took courage to have left the only home she remembered to strike out on her own at the young age of seventeen. She'd made the best of what life had offered to her. Surely she could see...

He got out of his chair and limped the few steps to the couch, where he sat down beside her. Her eyes grew larger as he moved closer.

And that was another thing. She had beautifully expressive, vulnerable eyes. He felt as though he could see through them to her soul.

Tony picked up her hand. She stiffened at his touch.

"Hey, relax. I'm not going to bite you, you know."

"Sorry," she muttered, leaving her hand on his palm.

"Don't you ever look in the mirror?" he asked softly.

"What?" Now she really seemed confused. "What are you talking about?"

"Don't you see how lovely you are?" He touched her cheek with his forefinger and discovered it felt every bit as soft as it looked, but the satiny smoothness surprised him. This close to her he could see golden flecks of color in her emerald eyes. Thick lashes framed them. He could count the smattering of freckles across her nose.

He smiled into her eyes. "You really are a beautiful woman," he said softly.

The poignant expression on her face almost unmanned him, causing a lump in his throat. He wasn't used to the surge of strong emotion that suddenly swept over him. Tenderly he slid his hand to the nape of her neck and gently eased her closer to him until their lips met.

Her lips were warm and quivering. This close, he was aware of her quick breathing. She was as still as a deer caught in the sudden headlights of a car.

Tony had a strong need to hold her in his arms, to keep her safe from a sometimes uncaring, thoughtless world.

He increased the pressure on her mouth ever so slightly. She didn't draw away, but she didn't relax her lips, either. A startling realization hit him; that she had never experienced a kiss.

She wasn't fighting him or trying to pull away. She seemed to be waiting to see what he would do next.

Tony drew away from her slightly, shifted his body and lifted her onto his lap, so that she was leaning against his shoulder with both of his arms securely around her.

He liked that much better. When he looked down at her, he discovered her eyes were closed. Her chest was quivering from the rapid beat of her heart. Come to think of it, his own heart had started pounding just as fast, despite the fact that they had done nothing more than press their lips together.

"Christina?"

Her thick lashes fluttered open and she gazed up at him. "I want to kiss you very much, but if you'd rather I didn't, I'd be content to just sit here and hold you, if you don't mind."

She licked her lips, a movement to which he reacted strongly. "I'm not very good at it," she admitted honestly.

That's when a crack appeared in the wall around his heart.

He stroked his tongue gently across her lips, enjoying the taste of her. "I could teach you," he offered lightly while he gauged her reaction to his touch.

"Okay," she whispered, so softly he wasn't certain whether he heard the words or just saw her lips move.

"I promise not to take advantage of you in any way. I'll stop whenever you want. Deal?"

She nodded, as though unable to verbally respond.

In his best instructor's tone, together with a teasing smile, he said, "Open your mouth for me, okay?"

She blinked in surprise, then obligingly dropped her jaw.

"Not quite that much." He adjusted her chin. "There." He took a deep breath. "Oh, yes. You got that just right." He closed his eyes and found her waiting lips with his, feeling another strong surge of desire rush through him.

When he brushed past her lips with his tongue, she stiffened at first, then slowly relaxed. She returned the pressure of his mouth and shyly touched her tongue to his.

Oh, yes.

Tony forgot that this was supposed to be a lesson of sorts, which wasn't surprising, since he was the one learning the most. She felt fragile in his arms, small boned and lightweight. He was afraid he could crush her if he weren't careful.

His body was ravenously enthusiastic, hardening with such intensity that he stiffened and pulled away from her, hissing through his teeth.

"Did you hurt your ankle?" she whispered, turning her head.

"Uh, no. Just got a cramp for a second. It's okay," he improvised.

Her face was flushed now, but not with embarrassment. Her eyes sparkled, looking like multifaceted gems glinting in sunlight. This woman was absolutely adorable. How could it have taken him so long to have recognized it?

He kissed her again. She immediately put what she'd just learned to use and kissed him back with unfeigned enthusiasm. She was so honest, hiding nothing of what she was feeling, and what she was feeling at the moment was strong sexual desire. He recognized it, since he was experiencing the same thing.

The difference was he knew where this was leading and she didn't. He had to cool it quickly or the situation was going to get out of hand.

When he attempted to pull away, she tightened her hold around his neck.

Another kiss wouldn't hurt, he convinced himself. Just one. The third kiss felt so natural he was certain that he'd been kissing this woman all of his adult life. Her mouth molded to his, her tongue dueled with his, her heart beat in the same rhythm as his.

He placed his hand just below her breast and she immediately arched toward him. He eased his hand upward until it cupped her small breast.

He'd been correct. She wore no bra, an incendiary discovery he could easily have done without. He brushed his thumb restlessly across the tip and felt it become pebble hard.

He heard her moan and knew that he had to stop...now...or his control would be gone.

Tony raised his mouth from hers and began to kiss her face, soothing her and him as well with a contact that didn't add fuel to their already overheated state.

He brushed his fingers through her hair, loving the springy wiriness that gave it a life of its own.

She clung to him, her face buried in his shoulder. He sat there holding her without any thought of time passing. He wondered about this woman-child in his arms. Who had held her like this when she was hurt, or scared or ill? Who had kissed her bruises, chased the bad dreams away, nurtured her?

Was that why she had provided a haven for her menagerie of strays, the discards of society? Because she knew what it was like to be alone in the world, unloved, unwanted?

His arms tightened for a brief hug, to let her know that he cared. He felt different, somehow, as though something had shifted in his view of life. He was at peace, even tolerant of the pets newly introduced to his usually well-ordered existence.

Which was just as well, since Minerva chose that moment to add her opinion. "'I will try to walk a blameless path, but how I need thy help!'"

He grinned, his chin resting on Christina's head. He felt her quiver, then heard her snicker. He threw his head back and laughed. She raised hers, caught his eye and burst into melodious laughter.

With his arms still around her, Tony basked in the moment, enjoying holding her and sharing her infectious laughter as much as he'd enjoyed making love to her.

With a brief flash of insight, he realized he was glad that Christina O'Reilly had set out to explore her genealogy. Otherwise, they might never have met.

Four

After lunch Tony suggested they ride into town. The house had become a provocative setting in his mind, a fact that dismayed him. He'd only met Christina the day before, hadn't even liked her when they met, and now he had to fight to keep his hands off her.

It should have made him feel a little better that she seemed as affected by what had happened to them that morning as he did. He felt like he'd been innocently crossing an empty railroad track when a train suddenly barreled out of nowhere and pulverized him.

He found himself gazing at her whenever she wasn't looking, then averting his eyes when she happened to glance at him ... which she seemed to be doing with unnerving frequency. He kept finding excuses to be near her, to touch her or to accidentally brush against her, and was thoroughly ashamed of himself for his behavior.

The trip to town was a desperate measure.

"You didn't go through Mason when you came here yesterday, did you?"

"No, why?"

"No reason. Sometimes I drive into town on Sunday, maybe get a bite to eat, check to see what's playing at the one movie house in town. I thought you might like to see the town where I grew up and went to school."

What a stupid thing to say. What made him think she'd care anything about where he went to school?

Her face lit up. "That sounds like fun." Then her smile faded. "But I don't think you should be trying to drive, do you?"

"My car's an automatic. I don't use it as much as the truck, but it will do it good to take it out on the road, blow some of the carbon out of the exhaust."

She glanced down at her clothing. "Should I change?"

"You wear whatever you want, honey-chile. You look just fine to me." And she did. My oh my, she looked good enough to snack on, and he could think of several places he'd like to—

Enough! Tony shoved his hand through his hair.

"Are you okay?" she asked. "Is your ankle bothering you?"

His ankle had been the last thing on his mind for the past several hours. Christina was certainly a great distraction for pain. Unfortunately, she'd created a new kind of discomfort, one so out of character for him that he was at a loss how to deal with it.

He felt like a bull pawing the ground to get into the pasture of a prime heifer. Boy, if his uncle Cody could see him now, he'd laugh his head off. He'd been telling Tony for years that he just hadn't met the right woman to ring his chimes for him, but that when he did, he'd be just like all the rest of them, following her around on a leash.

He wasn't *that* bad, of course. She'd just stirred him up a little, that's all. A drive would do him good.

"Is it all right to leave the animals inside?" she asked.

He eyed that walking demolition derby, Hercules, a little doubtfully. He hated to think about the possible damage the dog could do without trying.

As for Prometheus... "I dunno," he admitted. "What do you think?"

"Well, Minerva will be fine, of course. Prometheus has already checked out everything in the house and seems to have accepted it, but sometimes when they're left alone, he likes to tease Hercules. At least I think that's what happens, because I saw him tease Hercules into chasing him once, which explained why the house looked like a tornado had gone through it when I got home."

"We'll take Hercules with us," Tony decided recklessly. "He can sit in the back."

"You're sure?"

"Oh, yes."

"Or I could put him on a leash and tie him to the front porch."

"I have a hunch that if he decided to chase something, he'd take pillar, porch and all with him. No. He'll come with us."

Which was how Tony happened to spend the twenty-mile trip into town having the back of his neck licked by a grateful canine.

* * *

They stopped for coffee at the local Mexican restaurant and saw Clem visiting with a couple of his
friends. The shocked look on the man's face alerted
Tony to the very real possibility that Clem would accidentally reveal to Christina that this was the first
Sunday Tony had been to Mason since he was in high
school. He seated Christina in one of the booths and
excused himself for a moment. He stopped by Clem's
table and said hello to the others. To Clem he said, "I
thought I'd show her around a little. I'm supposed to
entertain her until the folks get back, which will be
another week."

Clem's brows rose. "A week? You're going to have
her and all them crazy animals around that long?"

"They aren't that bad once you get used to them. It
was all new to them at first, but they're settling in."

If possible, Clem's brows rose even higher. "You
feeling okay, Tony? Did you double up on your pain
pills or something?"

"No. The ankle's much better today."

"It ain't your ankle I'm a worryin' about. It's your
head. Do you think you got a concussion that we don't
know about?"

"Of course not."

"Well, you're shore actin' strange."

"The hell I am. I'm just entertaining my guest,
which means I've got to get back over there. Uh, in
case she says anything to you, I told her I often spend
my Sundays here in town. I didn't want her to think I
was making some special trip out of it. You understand?"

"Hell, no. I don't understand none of this, but if you're telling me to keep my mouth shut, that I can do with no problem."

Tony straightened, slapped him on the back and said, "Good. See you tomorrow." He rejoined Christina in the booth. Her eyes were shining.

"Would it be possible to look in the window of some of the shops along the square? This place reminds me of several of the small county towns scattered throughout the South. I'd love to go in some of the stores and look at things, but I noticed they're closed today."

"I have to come to town in the morning on business. If you want to ride in with me, you can look around while I'm at my meeting."

"Great idea. I love craft stores. They give me some great decorating ideas."

"Sure. No problem. We can—"

"Hey, Callaway! How come you brought one of your horses into town in the back of your car? Your truck-and-trailer rig broke down?"

Two of the locals had just walked through the door. Tony had grown up with both of them. He closed his eyes and gave a brief shake to his head. He knew without a doubt that he wasn't going to live this one down, no matter how long he tried.

He nodded when they walked up to the table. "Howdy, Jim... Pete. I'd like you to meet Christina O'Reilly. She's visiting with the family for a while. Christina, these two yahoos are the poorest excuse for linemen in all of Mason's illustrious football history."

"Yeah, right. If you had ever learned to get the ball off in decent time, we could have held 'em with no problem," Jim said.

Christina looked at Tony. "You played football?"

Pete whistled. "You mean ya haven't pulled out all your trophies and done a little bragging? You're slipping, boy."

"What position did you play?"

Before he could answer, Jim jumped right in. "Quarterback. He made quite a name for hisself when he was playing with the Aggies."

"Aggies?" she repeated.

"Texas A & M."

"So where'd you get the hoss in your car?"

"He belongs to me," Christina said with quiet dignity.

Immediately the joking around stopped, the men grew very polite and began to pay increasingly outlandish compliments with regard to Hercules's looks, size and heredity.

"You ready?" Tony asked Christina, knowing that these two characters weren't about to leave them in peace. They were having too much fun...at his expense.

"Sure. Whenever you are."

He knew everybody in the restaurant and they, of course, knew him. By the time Christina walked out of there, every one of them would have been able to describe her well enough for an artist to do a full-body composite of her.

The joys of living in a small town.

Instead of being irritated, he was amused. Part of the reason was that if he needed any kind of help at any time, he knew there wasn't a person in the place who wouldn't have leapt to his aid without hesitation.

The joys of living in a small town.

"So? Now what?" Tony asked when they got back to the car. Hercules was so excited to see them that the vehicle rocked with his enthusiasm.

"I think we're going to have to take him home, don't you?" she asked. "We'd better not risk seeing a movie."

"I think you're right. Clem will be at the ranch tomorrow and can keep an eye on him for us. For now, we'd do better to head on back."

By the time he could reasonably be expected to be tired enough to excuse himself for the night, Tony's body was humming with sexual tension.

They'd watched a couple of hours of television, interspersed with Minerva's singing psalms of thanksgiving and praise. Surprisingly enough, she sounded good. Christina explained, "Mrs. Bledsoe has a beautiful voice and used to sing around the house. I think that's how Minerva learned so much. She certainly didn't get it from me. As much as I love music, I can't carry a tune."

They were both working on keeping a casual conversation going, but the undercurrent in the room was twanging with tension. Tony knew that she must be as aware of him as he was of her. There wasn't a damn thing he could do about his reaction to her, either. He felt like he'd suddenly been fine-tuned to her frequency, and he kept picking up all kinds of messages that were driving him crazy.

She wasn't doing a thing to cause him to react this way. She wasn't flirting, fluttering her eyes, touching him, giggling or blushing. She was just being herself, and his body was going wild.

"I think I'm going to turn in. You go ahead and stay up if you'd like. The house is locked up. You'll be fine."

She got up and turned off the television. "That's all right. I'm a little tired myself. I'll go to bed, too."

There. He'd deliberately refrained from using the word *bed*. It provoked too many responses in him at the moment. Didn't she have any idea what he was going through? He was acting like some crazed animal.

"I'll keep Hercules with me," she said, starting down the hallway toward the guest room.

"You don't have to. As long as I know where he is, there won't be a problem."

She leaned against her door. "Okay. Sleep well. I hope your ankle's better by morning."

"Oh, it's practically well," he lied. "Good— Uh, would you mind if I gave you a good-night kiss?"

She flushed but she was smiling. "Sure. As you've probably guessed, I need the practice."

He wrapped his arms around her and pulled her up snug against his body. "Oh, I don't know," he murmured, nuzzling her throat and ear, "you're a real fast learner."

"Am I?" she whispered into his ear. "Is there more you want to teach me?"

His body jolted like he'd just been jabbed with an electric cattle prod. "Damn right there is," he muttered, nibbling on her earlobe.

"I'm always intrigued by the possibility of additional education," she murmured demurely.

He raised his head and eyed her. "You making fun of me?"

She chuckled. "Not at all! Rather, of myself. I'm woefully ignorant when it comes to men."

With his arms still around her, he leaned his back against the wall of the hallway, his legs braced apart. He pulled her into his body, knowing he was playing with fire but not caring. In that position he could feel every part of her pressing against every part of him. She was getting a post-graduate anatomy lesson standing right there in the hall.

"Haven't you ever had a boyfriend?"

Her head lay against his shoulder while her arms were looped around his chest. "Yes and no."

"What does that mean?" He rotated his hips and felt the soft material of her skirt rub against his hard and sensitive denim-clad flesh.

She mimicked his movement, causing such a riot of sensation that his knees quivered. She was learning much too fast for him to keep teasing both of them like this.

"That, uh, means that I've dated a few men, considered them friends, so in that respect I've had boyfriends."

"But no one serious?"

"Of course not."

"Why do you say it like that?"

"I'm not the type men get serious about," she explained patiently, as though to a slow-learning child.

"You're doing it again," he warned.

She pulled away from him and looked down into the narrow space between them. "Doing what?" she asked, puzzled.

He laughed and pulled her back to him by sliding his hands over her rump and lifting her into him. "Putting yourself down."

She looked at him in surprise, her expression even more puzzled. "No, I'm not. I'm just telling you the truth. I become every guy's pal, his buddy, his sister. He tells me his troubles with the woman in his life, or grouses about his ex or moans about his boss, but I certainly don't arouse him into seeing me as a romantic object."

"Oh, no?" he murmured, rubbing suggestively against her.

"But this isn't about you and me," she astounded him by saying, perfectly serious. "You just offered to teach me some things I don't know anything about." She stroked his cheek fondly. "And I appreciate it very much." She nuzzled her face into his chest. "This is wonderful."

Tony pushed her away from him so that he could see her face. "Do you mean to stand there and tell me you think this is some kind of advanced sex education we're doing here?"

She studied his face carefully before she asked, "Are you angry with me for some reason?"

Tony had an urgent desire to howl like one of the coyotes in the surrounding hills. "Angry? Me? Why should I be angry that you might think I would brutally and callously treat you like some sex object, a plaything to fondle and caress out of some insane need to drive myself out of my ever-lovin' mind?"

"This bothers you, what we've been doing?"

"You're damn right it 'bothers' me, or hadn't you noticed the steam shooting out of my ears?"

She cupped her hands over his ears and smiled up at him so warmly, so openly that the cracks splintered and shattered and the walls fell away from around his formerly guarded heart. "You're so sweet, Tony. I'm glad I got to meet you."

Sweet? Nobody had had the nerve to call him sweet since he was out of diapers.

The bottom line was that she didn't believe him. His kisses earlier today had awakened her, there'd been no doubt about that, and their sexual play here in the hallway had aroused her, still no doubt there. But she didn't understand that it wasn't just because she was female that he was breathing like a runaway steam engine. It was because of her, Christina O'Reilly of Atlanta, Georgia.

His frustration caused him to grab her and kiss her without pretense or apology. He put all of his own longing and formerly banked passion into it, telling her without words how much he wanted her, how he wasn't sure he could get through the night without taking her, that she was the sexiest, most seductive woman he'd ever come across.

By the time he eased away from her, she was limp and would have fallen if he hadn't held on to her. So he used that excuse to continue to hold her until she could slow her breathing and her heart rate.

"What am I going to do about you?" he murmured, more to himself than to her.

She lifted her face until he could look into her brilliantly gleaming eyes. "I'll only be here for a few days," she said, as though consoling him.

He straightened from where he'd been leaning against the wall once again, opened the guest-bedroom door and gently pushed her inside.

"That's what scares me," he said, closing the door.

He opened his own door and said, "Hercules? You coming to bed?" He heard a scrambling of feet, an ominous thud as though something had hit the floor, and the dog appeared in the hallway, looking delighted and eager. Tony pointed and the dog dashed past him, slid to an ungainly halt beside the bed and collapsed in a heap, his tongue lolling.

Tony shook his head and closed the door behind him. He must be out of his mind. He was actually becoming attached to this ridiculous animal.

He lay in bed for a long time before falling asleep, trying to come to some understanding of why he was becoming even more attached to Hercules's owner.

Christina floated over to the bed and sat down, staring into space. Today had been the most astonishing, wonderful, unbelievable day of her life.

She'd been kissed by Tony Callaway. She was still having trouble taking it in. Why had he spent so much time with her? Of course, he'd told his mother he'd look after her, which was kind of him. But he was being more than kind. He was being . . . ardent.

And that last kiss. Wow! It had turned her bones to water. She'd heard that expression before, but she wasn't sure she actually believed it could happen . . . until tonight.

If he hadn't been there to catch her, she would have melted into a puddle at his feet.

Her body was behaving so strangely. Parts of her that she'd never given much thought to were ultrasensitive and throbbing. She felt restless and languid at the same time. Most of all she hadn't wanted Tony to stop holding her and kissing her. She wanted to discover whatever came next, and next, and next. She wanted to experience the whole spectrum of what all of these sensations meant and how they played a part in a person's life. She knew that once she left here, she'd never have the opportunity to experience them again.

Tony didn't treat her like a buddy, a sister, a pal. No. He treated her like some movie-screen siren that drove him mad with desire. She hugged herself and laughed quietly with excitement at the thought. He wasn't faking his reactions. A man couldn't fake those kinds of physical responses.

The strangest part about the entire day was the surprising discovery that she didn't mind being touched and held by a man. Or was it only Tony? She didn't know and at the moment it didn't matter. She'd grown up knowing that there was something wrong with her. People were nice to her, they spoke to her, listened to her, complimented her. They just didn't touch her.

By the time she was a teenager she wasn't comfortable being touched. Once she started to date, her personal boundaries were obvious to any man who came around. If he ignored her wishes, she didn't see him again.

Tony was different and she didn't know why. She'd felt safe when he held her in his lap. Safe and seductive. Warm and wanton.

She could have done without Minerva's comment, but it had freed the tension between them. She'd been hiding her face, wondering how she was going to be able to look him in the eye. And then he had laughed, something she wouldn't have expected from this tough, hard man.

She loved his laugh. It was full of life. She wondered if he laughed often. Somehow she doubted it. The photographs sitting on the fireplace mantel revealed him to be a solemn child. Later snapshots taken with various family members invariably captured him staring into the camera without a hint of his so-attractive smile.

She hoped that her visit would add a little humor to his life. It would be nice to know that she'd made a difference to him. She knew that she would never be the same after meeting him. She wouldn't have missed it for the world.

Her mind calmed as her body eased into repose. Christina took a shower and changed into her thigh-length nightshirt. She stretched, then slipped into bed, smiling.

Tomorrow she would go to town with Tony. She wanted to repay his hospitality by doing something special for him, something he wouldn't do for himself.

She knew she had come up with a great idea that would remind him of her once she was gone. She drifted off to sleep, her head filled once again with wishes and dreams.

Five

Tony was jolted awake the next morning by a rough tongue being slapped across his face. He sprang into a sitting position, blinking in the pale dawn light.

Hercules sat and watched him expectantly.

"What? What do you want? Don't do that again, all right? Whatever you want, find another way to get my attention." He wiped the side of his face in disgust.

Hercules whined.

"You want out?" Tony guessed.

The dog stood up and whined.

All right. He could handle that. It was time to get up anyway. He fumbled for his jeans and slid them over his legs and hips. He padded barefoot to the bedroom door, eased it open and motioned Hercules through. He let him out the kitchen door and watched the dog bound across the ranch yard to investigate the row of cedars planted as a windbreak.

It was a shame to have a dog that size cooped up in a house in the city. No wonder Hercules sometimes expended some of his energy chasing the cat. Tony winced at a sudden vision of what the house would look like as a result.

Something soft brushed against his bare ankle. He glanced down and saw Prometheus. He didn't know where the cat had been or how he'd gotten outside. Maybe he could escape through closed doors, for all Tony knew.

The cat stalked past him, turned and rubbed against his leg once again.

"What is this? Are you trying to make friends with me?" Tony gingerly knelt, noting that his ankle felt much better this morning, even though it was now turning a vivid yellow and blue.

Prometheus stopped moving and watched him without blinking. "I don't know anything about cats," he said. The feline continued to stare at him. "You hungry?" No response. Tony held out his hand. Prometheus leaned forward and daintily sniffed, then regally lowered his head. Tony scratched tentatively behind his ear. A loud rumble emanated from the cat's chest.

Hercules came dashing back to the house, slinging legs and paws in all directions. With dignity, the cat leapt up on the porch railing and stared down at the large animal. They eyed each other thoughtfully, as though agreeing to meet on the field of combat at some future date.

Tony shook his head and ushered the dog back into the house. He put some coffee on and went to take a shower. He had a big day planned. The meeting at the bank would decide his immediate future. If he got the loan, he would be attending cattle auctions and buying stock. Without it, he would continue following the rodeo circuit this year, hoping for big-enough winnings to eventually buy the stock he needed.

One way or the other, he was going to get what he wanted without asking for help from the Callaway empire.

When Tony came out of his room dressed for his meeting, he heard voices in the kitchen. Christina's light, melodious tones interwove themselves with Clem's deeper ones.

Tony paused in the doorway. Christina had also dressed for town. She wore a demure shirtwaist dress in a soft yellow. Her shoes hid her colorful toenails. She'd pulled her hair back from her face into a French braid, although wiry tendrils resisted being subdued. She looked peaceful and composed, nothing like the seductive temptress that had filled his dreams.

"'Who can find a virtuous woman? For her price is far above rubies,'" Minerva announced from her new position in front of the kitchen window.

Clem grinned. "Mornin'," he said with a nod.

Christina jumped up. "How do you want your eggs?" she asked, gliding to the stove.

"Over easy." Tony sat down at the table and poured himself a cup of coffee.

"You made quite a stir in town yesterday," Clem said.

Tony glared at him over his cup.

"Oh, really?" Christina asked, glancing over her shoulder. "Why is that?"

Tony continued to watch Clem without blinking.

Clem drank from his cup before answering. "Not too many folks seen a dog that size before. Them that saw him had to describe him to them who didn't."

Tony allowed himself a small smile. Clem winked at him.

Christina returned to the table with Tony's plate. The eggs looked perfect—not lacy around the edges, not broken, not too hard. "Thanks," he said.

"You look very nice this morning," she said softly.

He almost choked on the bite of food he'd just placed in his mouth. He chewed carefully before saying, "Thank you."

Clem couldn't leave it alone. "I should say so," he added expansively, leaning back into his chair. "You look like you're going to a weddin', all suited up like that."

"When do we have to leave?" Christina asked in all innocence, catching Clem off guard.

"Wha—!" The front legs of his chair thumped as they hit the floor. "Are you—?"

Tony hastily interrupted. "Christina wants to look at some of the stores while I'm talking with Lin Schulz." He turned to her. "We need to leave in about half an hour." Once again he focused on Clem. "I'd like you to keep an eye on Hercules for us. He should be all right in the yard. If you go check on any of the pastures, take him along."

"Me?"

Tony looked at him coolly. "That's right."

Clem glanced at Christina. "Sure thing, Boss."

Nothing more was said through breakfast.

* * *

By the time they left Mason it was almost two o'clock. They'd stayed in town for lunch, indulging in sinfully delicious hamburgers from the local bakery-restaurant.

When Tony had come out of the bank, he'd found Christina near the car, peering into one of the art galleries on the square.

"Been waiting long?" he asked, coming up to her.

She spun around at the sound of his voice, smiling. "No. I just brought some of my purchases to the car and decided to wait here for you." She watched him expectantly. "Well?"

He shrugged. "I got my loan, but not as much as I wanted. He said he'd wait to see how things go this next year for me. If I can prove this will be a viable operation, he'll agree to loan me the rest."

"You should feel good about that."

He helped her into the car before he responded. "I guess. This is the first time I've ever asked for a loan. I don't like the feeling."

She looked at him in surprise. "Didn't you have to borrow for the ranch?"

He shook his head. "I used the earnings I'd saved up from the rodeo."

"Rodeoing must pay well."

"I was able to save most of what I got."

"Clem mentioned that you've won World Champion Bullrider three times."

"Clem has a big mouth."

"He's just proud of you."

"He can be proud and still have a big mouth."

She'd chuckled, and Tony had allowed himself a small smile.

He was glad to be heading home now so he could get out of his suit. He'd worn his dress shoes, the only pair he had, because his dress boots would have been too much for his ankle. He intended to spend the afternoon checking fences. He'd have Clem drive the truck for him.

He was surprised to see Clem coming from the barn as soon as they drove up. He wondered what Hercules had done this time. He hated to think about the possibilities.

Clem met them at the front door as Tony helped Christina carry in several packages.

"You had company this morning 'bout an hour after you left."

Tony heard a different tone in Clem's voice. When he glanced around, he saw that Clem's comment hadn't been addressed to him, but to Christina. She, too, paused and looked at Clem with a puzzled expression.

"Are you saying that *I* had company?" she asked. "How could that be? Nobody knows I'm here."

He shrugged. "I heard a car and thought you must've forgot something. I came out of the barn in time to see this green sedan pull up in front of the house and two men in suits get out. Of course, the great guard dog had to be pulled off 'em before I could find out what they wanted."

"Hercules attacked them?" She looked around. "Where is he, anyway?"

"Ah, he's plumb tuckered out after his strenuous morning greeting those guys. He 'bout licked 'em both to death with that giant tongue of his before I could get him inside the house."

"Did they say who they were and why they wanted Christina?" Tony asked. He followed her into the house and dumped his packages on the couch in the living room. Hercules dozed through their arrival, barely twitching his ear in acknowledgment of their presence.

Clem was right behind them. "Wouldn't say. Just asked if Christina O'Reilly was here and wanted to know when she would return. When I told them, they said they'd be back later."

"What did they look like?" she asked.

Clem shrugged. "Dark suits, red ties, short haircuts, polished shoes. I'd say government men."

"Why would they want to see me?" Christina asked.

"Since they weren't telling, if you don't know, I wouldn't either," Clem pointed out with a grin.

"How strange," she murmured.

"'Happy is the man that findeth wisdom and the man that getteth understanding.'"

"Thank you for that bit of enlightenment, Minerva," Tony said, shaking his head.

"'The Lord will not suffer the soul of the righteous to famish,'" she added.

"That's good to know," Tony replied. "But at the moment it doesn't give us much in the way of answers."

"If you'll excuse me," Christina said, "I'm going to change clothes. The only thing we can do is wait for them to come back and find out what they want."

Tony didn't like it. He had an uneasy feeling about the whole thing. Suppose it was somebody connected with the government. Why would they want to talk to

Christina? It must be important or they wouldn't have taken the time and trouble to track her down in Texas.

After all, how many people knew she'd come here?

Clem had gone back outside, and Tony decided to ask Christina. He tapped on her door. When she opened it, he realized that he'd caught her in the midst of changing. She held her robe in front of her, which was modest enough unless he looked beyond to where her backside was revealed in the full-length mirror across the room.

She wore a tiny pair of bikini panties that highlighted the smallness of her waist, the rounded flare of her hips and the delectable shape of her legs.

She wore no bra.

"Yes?" she asked, looking up at him.

He forgot why he'd knocked. He shut his eyes for a moment in an effort to erase the image he'd just witnessed. "I, uh—oh! I was wondering who knows where you are?"

"I've been thinking the same thing. I can't remember telling anyone, well, except for my next-door neighbor, who promised to water my garden while I was gone."

"Did you tell her specifically where you were going?"

"No, although I mentioned a few names—Allison Callaway in Austin, Trudi Flaherty in Corpus Christi, Jerome Kelly in Houston. They were just names I intended to look up."

"Jerome Kelly?" he repeated. "Who is he?"

"Another line from my great-grandmother. She had several brothers and sisters, and I've been—"

"Okay. But you haven't met him, have you?"

"I don't know if I can even find him . . . or Trudi. I wasn't certain I'd find Allison, either, for that matter."

"So whoever these men are, they've had to follow up on those names."

"I guess so."

He'd been conscientiously focusing on her face during their conversation. His concentration wandered, however, and he darted a glance into the mirror once more. Slender and sleek, like a race horse. He wanted to . . . "Uh, I'll let you get dressed then," he said, and watched in the mirror as she carefully adjusted the robe she clutched to her chest.

He felt like a damn Peeping Tom. He turned on his heel and said over his shoulder, "I think I'll check with Mom's housekeeper, Carlita, and find out if anyone showed up there asking about you."

Carlita quickly confirmed that two men had indeed arrived at his parents' home early that morning, asking for Christina. She had given them the same directions to his ranch as she'd given Christina.

"That's fine, Carlita, but do me a favor. If anyone else asks for her, tell them you don't know anything. Then call me immediately. Something's going on. I'm not sure what it is, but I don't like it."

"Oh, Mr. Tony, I'm so sorry. I didn't know what I should do. They were very serious, these men. I was afraid not to answer their questions."

"Don't worry about it. Whoever they are, I'll take care of them."

When he hung up, he decided not to check fences this afternoon. Instead, he and Clem would work around the ranch buildings, doing some needed repairs. There was always something breaking down.

* * *

After she closed the door on Tony, Christina quickly put on her oldest pair of jeans and a paint-spattered T-shirt. She could tell that Tony was worried about her visitors, but she wasn't. Whatever they wanted, it could have nothing to do with her. She lived a very quiet, uneventful life. She carefully obeyed all the rules and laws of the country.

She gathered up some of the items she had bought and headed for the kitchen. Actually, she was a very dull and boring person.

Once in the kitchen, she decided there was no reason why this room needed to be so dull and boring, however. What it needed was some color, and a little more light.

She looked around the utilitarian room. It spoke plainly of a man's lack of interest in decorating. Very little light came through the curtains at the window. Dingy walls looked neglected.

She smiled with anticipation. She could hardly wait to see Tony's face once he witnessed the results of her plans to transform this room.

Tony worked until almost dark before deciding to call it a day. There had been no sign of visitors. Had they decided not to return? Somehow he doubted it. They had gone to a great deal of trouble to find Christina. Now that they had, he felt certain they'd be back.

The question was when. He didn't like this waiting around and wanted to be there with her when they came. At the same time, he refused to examine this new protectiveness he was feeling toward her.

"I'm going into town for supper," Clem said, stripping off his work gloves, "as soon as I get cleaned up. That is, unless you think I should hang around, just in case.''

"Nah, go ahead. I can handle whatever it is.''

They looked at each other for a long moment before Clem nodded. ''See ya later, then.''

Tony was looking forward to a hot shower and a hot meal, not necessarily in that order. He took the back steps two at a time, strode across the porch and opened the screen door.

Only then did he come to a sudden halt and stare in stupification at the sight in front of him. His kitchen was gone. He gave his head a brief shake, deciding his mind was deceiving him.

"What do you think?'' Christina asked brightly.

Slowly he turned his gaze to hers. "It's... I can't tell you how... It's, uh, different. Real different.''

"I wanted to brighten everything up.''

"You managed to do that, all right.''

The truth of the matter was that Tony didn't remember the original color of his walls. They just sort of blended in with the rest of the kitchen.

Now they were a sparkling white, except for one that was covered in a colorful wallpaper print featuring blue-and-white ducks. The cabinets had also been painted bright white, with blue-and-white ducks appliquéd on the doors.

Ruffled curtains hung on either side of each window. The ducks were in evidence on the curtains as well.

"I had to make a choice between cows, pigs and ducks. I thought the ducks would look nice.''

He swallowed. Ruffles at the windows? He didn't want to think about Clem's reaction when he saw his

bachelor kitchen done up in blue-and-white ducks...
and ruffles.

"It, uh, looks a lot brighter," Tony offered lamely.
Damn, but he didn't want to hurt her feelings. She
looked like a little girl in her spattered shirt and jeans,
barefoot, with rainbow-colored toenails. She was so
blasted pleased with herself.

"I wanted to surprise you," she said shyly.

"Oh! Well, you certainly did that!" he quickly
agreed, finding a way to show his enthusiastic response to her efforts. He looked around the kitchen
once again. The room was much lighter, he had to admit. Of course, the tile floor looked old and worn in
comparison. It had all blended together before.

"I'm afraid dinner's going to be a little late tonight. I lost track of the time. I wanted to be finished
before you returned to the house."

"Don't worry about it. I'll get washed up while
you're heating up something. There's probably something in the freezer already made up from last week."

She followed him into the hallway. He paused in the
living room to toss down his hat and work gloves. She
came up behind him and said, "You don't mind that
I decided to change your kitchen without asking you,
do you?"

He turned and met her green eyes, which were filled
with worry.

He didn't care about his blasted kitchen, one way or
the other. It served its purpose, as far as he was concerned. But if she wanted to change it, she could
change it.

He looped his arms around her waist and drew her
to him, pleased at how well their bodies aligned to
each other. "I'm touched that you went to so much

work for me. I want to pay you for all your supplies. I want to show you how much I appreciate your efforts.''

Her face lit up in a mischievous smile. She slipped her arms around his shoulders and went up on tiptoe. ''I'm ready for my next lesson,'' she whispered, brushing her lips against his. ''That is, if you're up to it.''

''Honey-chile,'' he drawled, ''I always seem up to it whenever you're around.'' He touched her eager lips with his, his tongue invading, teasing her, teasing them both with its suggested rhythm and primitive possession.

'' 'Mercy and truth have met together. Grim justice and peace have kissed!' ''

Tony released his tight hold on her and allowed Christina to lean against him while they both worked to catch their breath. He waited until he could speak without panting, then said, ''I have only one question. Am I grim justice or peace?''

Her answering laugh reassured him as he made his escape down the hall to his room.

All the while he was in the shower, Tony lectured himself on his behavior. Christina was a guest in his house. As her host, he had a responsibility not to take advantage of her. She had no idea what she was asking as she teasingly requested lessons in lovemaking. The problem was that he knew exactly what such lessons would entail. If he had any doubts, his dreams graphically reminded him.

He liked Christina. How could anyone not like such a warm, openhearted, personable woman? She deserved better than to get her lessons from a battered cowboy whose focus remained on ranching and rodeoing.

Besides, he wouldn't be able to look his mother in the face when she returned if he took advantage of the situation they were in this week.

Six more days, that's all he had to get through. Six more days. Six more days... and nights. He could do it. Of course he could. However, he'd have to limit himself to an arm's-length relationship. Any closer and he promptly forgot all his good intentions.

They had finished dinner and were putting away the last of the dishes when he heard a knock at the front door.

"Wait here," Tony instructed Christina. He strode to the door and opened it.

The men looked much as Clem had described them, both of indeterminate age, nothing conspicuous or unusual about them.

"Yes?" he asked.

"We would like to speak to Ms. Christina O'Reilly," the blue-eyed one said.

"Why?" Tony asked bluntly.

"Is she here?" the brown-eyed one asked politely.

"It's all right, Tony," she said from behind him. She stepped around him. "I'm Christina."

Blue eyes nodded. "Hello, Ms. O'Reilly. My name is John Malone and this is Sam Johnson." He reached into his pocket, as did the other man. Both held out something toward her. She leaned closer, saw their names and faces and an official emblem stating Treasury Department.

Malone said, "We'd like to ask you some questions, if you don't mind."

"What about?" Tony asked.

Johnson said, "Would you mind if we come inside?"

Tony minded out of general principles. What did the Treasury Department want with Christina? However, they weren't here to see him and he grudgingly admitted to himself that this was none of his business.

However, he might very well decide at some point to make it his business. He glanced down at Christina and saw that she was waiting for him to invite them in, which he did rather begrudgingly.

She led the way to the couch and chairs. "Please be seated," she said, sounding like a gracious hostess. The men chose the matching armchairs facing the couch.

"We'd like to speak to you in private if we may," Malone said, causing Tony, who still stood near the door, to bristle.

"Please. I'd much rather have Tony with me, if you don't mind," she said quietly, giving him a beseeching look.

He immediately wanted to grab his armor and sword and charge into battle for her. He contented himself with walking over and taking her hand.

Johnson said, "You're Tony Callaway?" he asked, as though reading from some mental file.

"That's right."

Malone asked, "Cole Callaway's son?"

"Yes."

Malone allowed himself a brief smile. "I happen to know your father. He's a tough adversary, but a good man."

"Yes."

Malone and Johnson looked at each other. Johnson shrugged. Malone said, "I don't suppose it matters, if she wants him here."

"That's a relief," Tony muttered sarcastically. He nudged Christina to sit down on the couch. He sat down beside her, still holding her hand.

"What is your connection with the Callaways?" Malone asked.

"None," she began, but Tony interrupted.

"What does it matter to you guys? She's visiting with me for the week until my parents return from vacation. Exactly why have you gone to the trouble of looking for Christina?"

Malone reached into his inside coat pocket and pulled out a small notebook. He flipped it open and cleared his throat.

"I understand you used to work at the Federal Commerce Bank in Atlanta. Is that correct?"

"Yes."

"We'd like to know the circumstances under which you left the bank."

"Why?" Tony demanded.

Christina squeezed his hand. "I don't mind telling you, even though I'm a little sensitive about the circumstances. I've never been fired before."

Tony watched the men make eye contact with each other once more.

"What reason were you given for being fired?"

"I was told my work wasn't up to the bank's standards," she said in a quiet voice.

"Who told you this?"

"The head of accounting."

Johnson looked at the notebook he'd pulled out of a pocket. "That would be Marvin Leroy Thomas?"

"That's correct."

"Why do you care about all of this?" Tony wanted to know.

"We have reason to believe that someone working in the Federal Commerce Bank in Atlanta was laundering money through the bank. From what we've been able to uncover, Christina O'Reilly might be the one person who could give us details we need to build a case against them."

Six

Tony turned and looked at Christina. Her face registered her shock. He turned back to the men, who were watching her response just as intently.

"Do you mean you didn't know?" Malone asked gently.

Her eyes looked huge in her pale face. Tony slipped his arm around her protectively. She shook her head. "I had no idea."

"It's our guess that your dismissal was tied up in some way with this matter. Were you given severance pay?"

"Only what the law stipulates."

"Did anyone else at the bank discuss your employment with you? Were you given any other warnings about your performance before you were asked to leave?"

She thought about his questions before answering. "No. I had no idea. In fact, I'd gotten a merit raise the month before. I arrived at work Monday morning, as usual. I was generally the first one in the office. I had a routine of turning on the machines, making coffee, that sort of thing, and—"

"You say you were early?"

"Yes, sir."

"According to your personnel file, one of the reasons cited for your dismissal was your habitual tardiness."

"But that's not possible. My working hours were eight to five. I caught the same bus each morning, which dropped me off in front of the bank at twenty minutes before eight. I was always on time."

"What about absenteeism?"

"I think I missed three days in the five years I worked there."

Johnson was making notes while Malone directed the questions. "I see."

"Did they say something about that as well?" she asked.

"They noted an excessive amount of absenteeism."

Christina rubbed her forehead. "I don't understand."

"I think we can build a strong case, but we'll need you to work with us. You are our key witness because you had access to the accounts in question. What we'd—"

Christina gasped, her hand flying to her mouth. "Are you talking about the five accounts I found misidentified in the computer?"

"Five, did you say? We've only found two so far."

"There were five that had been erroneously cata-logued. At least, that's what I thought."

"Did you check with anyone before changing them?"

"No. I generally just go ahead and do whatever I think needs to be done. Most employers have praised my initiative."

Tony recalled his new, brightly painted kitchen. Yep, initiative was definitely one of her strong suits.

Malone closed his notebook and leaned forward so that his elbows rested on his knees. "Ms. O'Reilly, I don't want to alarm you, but what you did affected a money-laundering scheme that seems to be working along the eastern seaboard. From what you've told us you inadvertently stumbled across a highly sophisti-cated system that has taken years to put into place. We have a large number of people working on this thing. It would be very helpful if you would be willing to come back to—"

"No."

Three pairs of eyes turned to Tony.

"She's staying right here."

"I'm afraid you don't understand," Malone said with the beginning of strained patience. "We need her help. If she can help us identify anything with regard to—"

"What you're suggesting could get her killed."

"Well, as to that, we're prepared to make certain that she remains safe."

"So am I, and I'm her best bet in this deal."

"I don't follow you," Malone replied, no longer hiding his impatience.

"The first thing we have to do is contact her friendly neighbor and tell her to just water the damn garden

and keep her mouth shut. If anyone else comes looking for her, they won't have any idea where she is."

"How did you know—" Johnson began.

"Because she told me that her neighbor is the only
person who knew where she was going. Mrs. Bledsoe
only knew she'd be out of town for a few weeks. Since
Christina isn't working, she has no reason to return to
Atlanta any time soon, which is the safest course for
her at the moment."

Johnson rubbed his jaw, thinking. "He's got a good
point, John," he said, thoughtfully. "We had the
dickens of a time finding her, remember?"

"It didn't take you all that long," Tony pointed out.
"She's only been here for three days."

"Yes, but I left Atlanta two weeks ago," she said.
"I took my time traveling along the coast and seeing
new areas of interest."

"We started looking about ten days ago," Malone
said. "To be honest, your disappearance was what
alerted us that there might be something going on."

"What do you mean?" she asked.

"When the bank filed its quarterly reports with the
government, we saw a couple of unusually large accounts that hadn't been reported in previous quar-
ters. When we sent a routine inquiry, we were told that
the reports filed had been wrong, that no such accounts existed, that the error was due to incompetent
help in the accounting department, which had since
been corrected. A few days later another report was
filed that matched the previous ones."

"You didn't believe them?" she asked.

"Let's say we were a little curious, especially when
you're talking about those kinds of numbers. We decided to do some independent checking. During a

routine bank-examiners audit we went in and got the names of everyone who'd worked in the accounting department who'd left during the past twelve months and then looked them up to interview them. When we got to your name, we figured you were the one they'd been referring to. Then we discovered you'd gone, and your neighbor said you hadn't been sure when you'd be back.''

"But I could still have been an incompetent employee who'd been terminated.''

"That's true, except the bank examiners found a number of interesting discrepancies in the area they'd been told to carefully inspect. Although we gave the bank the impression everything was in order, we came away with bits of information that we've been piecing together. They're forming a very interesting picture.''

Christina turned to Tony. "This is exciting. I want to go back and—''

"No,'' he said firmly. "The professionals are handling it now, leave it to them. You stay out of it.''

"I suppose it would be possible to work with her here in Texas. I think you're right. It would be much safer. Once we start filing indictments, we'd need to place her in protective custody until time to testify.''

"When would that be?'' Tony asked.

"We can't be certain at this point, of course. We want to have a foolproof case before we go after these guys. With the kind of money involved, they can pull in some heavy artillery.''

"Your mother isn't going to want to be bothered with—'' Christina began.

"You'll stay here,'' Tony stated emphatically. "You will be with me. From now until this thing is concluded, I'm going to be your shadow, understand?''

She didn't, he could tell, but that didn't matter, as long as she accepted what he was saying. "But, Tony—"

"We can discuss it later." He turned to the men across from him. "Is there anything else you need to discuss with her tonight?"

"A few things, yes. If you could tell us about the files you saw and anything at all that you remember about them. With you working with us, I think we'll be able to move ahead faster, knowing what to look for. So far no one at the bank is suspicious of the investigation, which makes our job easier."

Tony stood and stretched. "Why don't all of you go into the kitchen, where you can spread out your notes and things," he said expansively, now that he'd gotten his own way without argument. "I'll make some coffee and leave you to discuss the details."

Malone looked at him in surprise. He, too, stood. "I appreciate that, Mr. Callaway. Your cooperation will make all of this a little easier."

"Glad to oblige. Just as long as you understand that Christina is my one-and-only concern in this matter."

Malone gave him a very masculine smile. "I would never have guessed."

Almost two hours later, Christina showed her visitors to the door and returned to where Tony was sprawled on the couch watching television, Prometheus on his chest.

He watched her walk toward him.

"You look comfortable."

"I am. So how did it go?"

She sat down in one of the chairs across from him. "Very well." She leaned back with a sigh. "Isn't all of this amazing? I wouldn't have dreamed that I would ever be mixed up in something so exciting.''

''You sound almost pleased.''

''Well, I am. I never expected to stumble across something like this in real life. This is the stuff of television movies.''

Tony lifted the cat off his chest and sat up. Prometheus promptly stepped on his leg and stretched out the length of his thigh. Tony frowned at the animal but left him where he was. ''The part to remember, Christina, is that this isn't a movie. There are some really dangerous people out there who are going to become more dangerous when this operation comes to light.''

She shivered, knowing he was right. Mr. Malone and Mr. Johnson had both warned her of the potential danger, but there was no question in her mind about what she had to do. What amazed her was how quickly she recalled the details of her job. She had been able to answer their questions with specific names as well as remember who had access to certain accounts, how she had stumbled across them and the system she had used to be able to correctly track them.

Mr. Malone had expressed his admiration for what she had done and said he'd certainly be glad to offer his recommendation when she looked for another job.

''Did they say when they might return?'' Tony asked.

''No. Just that they would be in touch. Mr. Malone gave me his card. He said for me to call him when I leave here.''

''You aren't going anywhere,'' Tony stated firmly.

She wondered if he had any idea just how gorgeous he was with his hair rumpled and his eyes so sleepy-looking. She had the strongest urge to wrap herself around the man and never let go.

"I can't stay here indefinitely," she pointed out.

"Why not?"

"If nothing else, I need to look for another job in a few weeks. I can't live off my savings forever."

"Do you miss working?"

"I never think about it. It's part of what I do to live."

"What I mean is, if you married, would you want to work?"

"I don't expect to marry, but if I did, I certainly wouldn't expect my husband to support me."

"What do you have against marriage?"

"Nothing. I'm just not the type of woman that causes a man to think about marriage."

"There you go again with your ridiculous assumptions. "'Not attractive enough,'" he mimicked. "'Not the type.' You've got to stop sticking labels on yourself like that."

"I just don't kid myself about who I am, that's all. I'm very happy with my life. I've created a home that's comfortable. I have my pets, my hobbies, a career.... Well, maybe career's too strong a word, but I'm qualified to hold a well-paying job. I'm healthy. I have everything I want."

"Haven't you ever wanted someone to love?"

She looked at him a little uncertainly. "What kind of question is that?"

"Someone who loves you, protects you, cares what happens to you. Haven't you ever dreamed about a time when you'd be the most important person in another person's life?"

"Have you?"

He straightened, as though unprepared for his questions to be tossed back at him.

He rubbed his chin. "Yeah...there are moments when I've given some thought to the idea. I don't have any particular time frame in mind, and I wanted to get the ranch built up a little more, but yeah, I want to get married someday."

Christina felt a sense of sadness seep through her. This man had so much to give someone. She bet there were dozens of women who were waiting to become that special someone in his life. She could almost see them in her mind's eye—beautiful women with luscious bodies all having the knowledge they needed to keep him dazzled with their allure.

She pushed up from her chair and said, "I'm sure it will happen when you're ready," she said wistfully. "I can't imagine any woman foolish enough to turn you down. I think I'm going to go to bed. I've had a rather exhausting day, all things considered. I'll see you tomorrow."

Tony watched her walk away, her slim back straight, her graceful stride reminding him of a danccr.

What had he said to make her look so sad? he wondered. Did she think he was becoming too personal, asking her so many pointed questions? As far as that went, he wasn't certain why he was so interested in her answers.

All he knew was that this woman had come into his life like a miniature tornado—her and her menagerie—and his life was still spinning.

Now he had T-men at his door, blue ducks with matching ruffles in his kitchen, a three-legged cat on his knee, a giant dog trailing him around and a bird that was doing her best to save his soul.

His previous life, from his present perspective, now appeared to him as a little dull. Absently he placed the cat on the couch beside him, stood and snapped his fingers at Hercules. It was time for a quick run around the yard and then bedtime. He'd had a fairly eventful day himself.

Hours later, his first thought was that he was in the middle of a horrendous earthquake. Not only was there booming, thunderlike noise and a keening wail nearby, but one of the heavy beams in the ceiling must have fallen, trapping him in the ruins of his bed.

One moment he'd been dreaming about Christina, about holding her in his arms, kissing and caressing her, then bam! The world had gone crazy.

He was trying to get his breath, wondering what could have caused such an event here in the Texas hill country, when his bedroom door flew open and Christina came dashing in, exclaiming, "Oh, no! I should have warned you. Oh, Hercules, look what you've done!"

The keening wail continued, almost drowning out her words.

She turned on the light, and Tony, in his dazed condition, thought it odd that the electricity was working. He could still hear her voice amidst the noise. "Get off him, do you hear? You're too heavy to lay on anybody. Haven't I explained all of this to you before?"

The beam across his middle shifted, then moved, and Tony took his first deep breath in what seemed like hours. He lay at a drunken angle, his feet higher than his head, and peered up at her.

She ran around the bed and knelt beside him. That's when he realized that part of the bed was now on the floor.

"What happened?" he asked.

Another crash of thunder sounded overhead and Hercules frantically scrambled to burrow beneath him.

"I should have warned you," Christina explained, clearly upset. "I just wasn't expecting a storm. Do they always come up so quickly here in Texas? If I'd had any idea..."

Tony shoved the dog away. "Stop that, you idiot hound. What's gotten into you, anyway?"

"He's afraid of thunder," she said. "Whenever we have a storm he tries to get into my lap or under the table. I've tried to explain to him that it's just noise and perfectly harmless, but he won't listen."

Tony pushed himself awkwardly up off the mattress, which was a little difficult, since his feet were still tangled in the sheets at a forty-five-degree angle above his head. After he got them free, he rolled to the edge and got up, looking down at the ruins of his bed.

"He must have gotten frightened and tried to get in bed with you."

Tony lifted the mattress and spring and saw that one of the slats had fallen, another one had snapped in two. "How much does he weigh, anyway? This bed should have held both our weights."

Christina stood as well. "I think he must have gotten a running start and leaped. He did that once to one of my chairs and it collapsed beneath him."

Tony turned and looked at the dog, who currently had his head under the covers and was still emitting a shrill, keening noise.

"Enough, Hercules," he said sternly. "Now shut up!"

The noise stopped, but the violent trembling continued.

"He's really frightened, isn't he?" Tony said in amazement. He shook his head in disbelief. "A would-be guard dog who welcomes everyone he meets and has a phobic fear of storms." He turned to Christina, and for the first time since she'd rushed in, he noticed what she was wearing—a nightshirt that stopped at midthigh. There was a giant panda on the front with the words *Hug Me*.

He grinned and followed instructions.

"What are you doing?" she gasped as he picked her up in his arms.

"Taking advice from your panda." He paused in the doorway, and after a brief glance back at the whimpering dog still huddled in the remains of his bed, he turned off the light. Crossing the hall, he entered the guest room and closed the door. She hadn't bothered to turn on a light in her mad dash to save him from possible suffocation. Other than the sporadic flickering of lightning from the storm passing overhead, the room was dark.

Tony didn't care. He knew where the bed was. He made his way carefully to its side, then sat down before rolling them both onto its surface. He gathered up the sheet and covered them.

"Have you lost your mind?" she squeaked.

"Not at all. Since your dog just destroyed my bed, I think it only fair that you share yours with me."

"Oh!" She was quiet. He wished he could see her face. Since he still held her in his arms, he knew that she wasn't afraid of him. Her body felt relaxed and

The TV is by Panasonic, and loaded with features! It has a high contrast 13" picture tube, comes with a remote control with on-screen displays. This TV even has a sleep timer! All in all, it's terrific! We'll be giving away 50 free TVs to prompt respondents. And we'll send you one, just for being picked as one of the fastest to reply!

Affix sticker to front of reply card and mail promptly!

◄ Claim your free books, free gift and try for a free Color TV today! Return this card promptly! ►

FREE TVs GIVEAWAY!

Here's a chance to get a free Color TV! And here's a chance to get **four free Silhouette Desire® novels** from the Silhouette Reader Service™!

We'll send you four free books so you can see that we're like **no ordinary book club!** With the Reader Service, you never have to buy anything. You could even accept the free books and cancel immediately. In that case you'll owe nothing and be under no obligation!

Thousands of readers **enjoy** receiving books by mail. They like the home delivery ... they like getting the novels **months before** they're available in bookstores ... and they love our **discount prices!**

Try us and see! Peel off the label from the TV above and stick it on the front of this reply card in the space provided. Be sure to fill in your name and address below and RETURN YOUR CARD PROMPTLY! We'll send you your free books and a free gift, under the terms explained on the back. And we'll also enter you in the drawing for the Free Color TV's (SEE BACK OF BOOK FOR FREE TV DETAILS). We hope that you'll want to remain a subscriber—but the choice is always yours.

225 CIS AQ4Z
(TVL-S-10/94)

Name _____

Address _____

City _____ State _____ Zip Code _____

☐ NO. Do not send me four books and a gift. Enter me into the Fast TV draw.

Book offer not valid to current Silhouette Desire subscribers. All orders subject to approval.

HERE'S HOW THE READER SERVICE WORKS. Accepting free books places you under no obligation to buy anything. You may keep the books and gift and return the shipping statement marked "cancel." If you do not cancel, about a month later we will send you 6 additional novels, and bill you just $2.44 each plus 25¢ delivery and applicable sales tax, if any.* That's the complete price—and compared to cover prices of $2.99 each, quite a bargain! You may cancel at any time, but if you choose to continue every month we'll send you 6 more books, which you may either purchase at the discount price ...or return at our expense and cancel your subscription.

*Terms and prices subject to change without notice. Sales tax applicable in N.Y.

Office use only

: /

POSTAGE WILL BE PAID BY ADDRESSEE

BUSINESS REPLY MAIL
FIRST CLASS MAIL   PERMIT NO. 717   BUFFALO, NY

SILHOUETTE READER SERVICE
FAST TV SWEEPSTAKES OFFER
P.O. BOX 9010
BUFFALO, NY 14240-9935

NO POSTAGE
NECESSARY
IF MAILED
IN THE
UNITED STATES

If offer card is missing, write to : Silhouette Reader Service, 3010 Walden Ave., P.O. Box 1867, Buffalo, NY 14269-1867

immensely pleasurable. He draped his leg over both of hers and sighed with satisfaction.

"I can sleep on the couch," she offered after a moment.

"That won't be necessary," he reassured her politely, glad she couldn't see the smug grin he couldn't seem to wipe off his face. "This is just fine."

She gave a little wiggle of adjustment, which brought her body more securely against him. Her head rested on his shoulder. He rubbed his chin against her cheek, still smiling.

"I've never attempted to sleep with anyone before," she said after a moment.

"Really? You have no idea what you've been missing."

She was silent for several minutes before she said, "You've probably slept with lots of people, haven't you?"

"Not lots, no. And not people as a class. A few...a very few...females."

He knew that to be a lie. He'd never slept with a female before. He might have been in bed with one, but he never fell asleep. He liked waking in his own bed, even if it was in a rented motel room. He liked waking up alone, but he didn't mind making an exception in this case.

In fact, he could get used to going to sleep wrapped around this particular female real easy. Almost addicting, it was.

Now that he was awake, though, he was wide awake. He must have had several hours of sleep before the storm blew into the area. Not only was he wide awake, but his body was stirring with anticipation.

"Tony?" she whispered.

"Mm?"

"Doesn't this bother you?"

"What?"

"Lying so close like this?"

"What do you mean, bother?"

"I just think that since this bed is so big, we could probably lie far enough apart that we wouldn't have to touch."

"That's true."

"Wouldn't you rest better that way?"

"No doubt."

She raised her head and tried to push away from him by placing her hands on his chest. Since his mother hadn't raised a fool, Tony left his arms around her. She was firmly anchored to his side by his leg across hers as well.

Christina brushed her hand across his chest in a smooth caress that made him want to purr. "Don't you want to rest?" she finally asked.

"Not particularly. Given the choice, I'd much rather hold you."

"Oh."

Minutes marched along in silence.

She stroked his chest again, as though exploring the contours. He trailed his hand down her spine, sliding it beneath the hem of her nightshirt and being rewarded by the feel of her satiny skin just above the waistband of her bikini panties. He caressed the slender indentation of her spine, tracing it slowly back to her neck.

She stirred restlessly and rubbed her cheek against his neck. He nipped her earlobe and was rewarded by a shiver. When she moved her head, he found her mouth, open and willing. He couldn't contain a groan of pleasure at her response. His mouth molded and shaped itself to hers and he nibbled her bottom lip, then soothed it with his tongue.

He moved his hand to her hip, then around to her stomach. She sucked in her breath when he trailed his fingers up to her breast.

"They're too small," she whispered sadly.

"No. They're perfect. See?" He wrapped his hand carefully around her. "They fit perfectly in my palm as though they belong there." He moved to the other one, rocking his hand back and forth over the tip until it stood erect.

Her breath made a whooshing sound as though she'd been holding it too long.

"Am I hurting you?"

"Oh, no."

"Do you want me to stop?"

"Oh, no!" She gave a breathless chuckle. "That feels so—so... I don't know how to describe it," she whispered, a little breathless.

"Me, either. I just know that I love holding you, touching you, kissing you. I can't seem to get enough of it." As if to prove his words, he began to kiss her again, as though he'd been deprived long enough of the taste of her lips.

He shifted his leg and rolled onto his back, pulling her on top of him. He loved feeling her light frame resting against him. He was also giving her control of the situation.

As though freed by his unspoken invitation, she explored his shoulders and chest with her hands and lips, sliding down his body and stroking the taut muscles of his abdomen.

His briefs could no longer contain his arousal, the elastic band causing him some discomfort. He reached down to make an adjustment and her fingers followed him, brushing his away and soothing the distended flesh.

He couldn't control the involuntary spasm that her touch caused him. She tugged the briefs down his legs and eased them off before returning to her exploration of him. There wasn't a hint of self-consciousness in her movements, just one of wonderment and new discovery.

Her touch was so gentle that there were moments when he felt like he was experiencing the flutter of butterfly wings wafting across his skin. He shuddered and forced himself to lie quietly. It was almost as though he were seeing himself from a brand-new perspective as a result of her innocent and guilt-free exploration and discovery of his maleness.

Her hands cupped his hardness and she placed a kiss very tenderly on his heated flesh, as though in benediction and acknowledgment of the basic difference between them.

A sudden jolt of unexpected emotion caused tears to spring to his eyes. He'd never experienced such an honest expression of appreciation from one human being to another. He was at a loss as to what he could do or say, and so he continued to lie there, waiting and watching her shadowy figure move above him.

By the time she touched her fingers against his cheek once more, she had explored every inch of his body, as though she'd needed to learn his anatomy through touch. Her words, when she spoke, shattered him with their sweet simplicity.

''Will you make love to me?''

Seven

The shock went through his body, and if possible, he became more rigid. He rested his hand on her hip as she stretched over him once again.

"Are you sure that's what you want?" he asked hoarsely.

"More than anything in my entire life," she replied.

Another wave of undiluted emotion swept over him. This time the tears trickled down his cheeks. He didn't bother wiping them away.

"Ah, Christi, you're something else." His voice broke.

"What's wrong?"

"Nothin'. You've just knocked down all my walls and crept past my defenses until all I can think about, dream about, is you."

"Really?" She sounded delighted.

"You've got me going in fifteen directions at once."

"Is that a yes or a no?"

"I want you so bad I ache with it."

"That sounds like a yes."

"I can't take your innocence."

"That sounds like a no."

"Don't ask this of me."

"You won't be taking anything. You'll be giving to me. I want my first time to be with you. You are so beautiful."

Tony had a lot of trouble with that. Nobody had ever called him beautiful. In fact, he would have decked almost anyone who ever did. Worse than that, she had said she wanted her first time to be with him. Knowing he would be the first didn't come as any surprise. He already knew that, but the way she said it bothered him. He didn't mind being the first, but he wanted to be the last and all the in betweens as well. He didn't want this beautiful woman-child to ever share herself with anyone but him.

The realization of what that meant scared the holy hell out of him.

When he didn't answer her, she moved away from him so that they were no longer touching.

"Where do you think you're going?"

"I got my answer. I'm going to let you go to sleep."

"Christi—honey-chile, what you're witnessing is the toughest struggle a man ever had with himself. If I win I lose and if I lose I lose, so I'm in trouble whichever way I decide." He turned on his side so that he was facing her. "The thing is, I want to make love to you more than anything I know."

She slid over to him and hugged him. "Show me," she said softly.

"But if I do, I've got to go back to my room for protection. That's a rule I never break."

"Because of what happened with your mom and dad?"

"How did you know about that?"

"From Clem."

"I told you he talks too much."

"It helped me to understand you better, I think. To understand why you're so independent."

"I love my dad. Don't ever doubt it. But I've got to live my own life and live it my way, not his. I also don't want to make the mistakes he made."

"You consider yourself a mistake?"

That stopped him. "Not exactly, but it sure made things tough on my mom."

"I don't know why your dad didn't learn about you for all those years, but if your mom had to lose him, at least she had you."

"That's what she told me."

"That's the way I would feel in her place. You couldn't be anybody's mistake, Tony Callaway. You're a very special gift."

Tony rolled away from her, off the bed, and strode into the other room. He found Hercules curled up in his bed, snoring slightly. Shaking his head, he fumbled in the drawer of his bedside table, grabbed the packets and went back to the guest room.

"You're the special gift, Christi," he whispered as he lay down beside her once more and pulled her into his arms. "I don't deserve you, but I want you so much, more than I've ever wanted anyone."

The talking was over, the decision made. Tony had done what he could to resist the temptation of her candid request, but he succumbed to his humanness and his burning desire to show this woman what love-making could be.

This time it was his turn to discover all the lush curves and planes of her body. His silent instruction was followed by her equally silent response as he lifted her nightshirt and she pulled it over her head. With a flick of his wrist he removed her panties so that he was free to memorize every quivering inch of her.

By the time he was kneeling between her knees, she was reaching for him, silently commanding him to take her—now!

He took his time, forcing himself to prepare her for his possession. When he'd finally broken through her barrier and buried himself within her, they were both shaking.

She placed frantic little kisses over his face, almost sobbing with the need for relief. In his concern to make certain she was ready, perhaps he'd pushed her too close to the edge without her understanding what was happening.

When he started moving within her, she quickly met him with eager thrusts of her own. Then, as though she suddenly understood, she gasped and clung to him, panting and pressing kisses on his chin and neck.

Her spontaneous contractions triggered his already overtaxed system and he felt as though he'd exploded into pieces of pure pleasure. He clung to her in dazed wonder, unable to comprehend what had just happened to him. He didn't want to let her go. Not now, not ever. She had become a part of him. In claiming her, he had claimed a part of himself he'd never known existed.

Her blissful sigh as she fell asleep snuggled in his arms brought a smile to his lips. Her wholehearted acceptance of him humbled him and made him feel unworthy.

He lay there listening to her soft, even breathing, attempting to cope with the rush of feelings he'd experienced. It was as though he now understood many things about life that had puzzled him in the past.

For the first time, he could understand what had happened between his parents so many years ago. He finally understood how they must have felt about each other, and with this new awareness, he was able to forgive.

Christina moved and Tony reflexively tightened his hold on her so that she continued to lie closely against his side. He didn't want to move from this wonderfully relaxing place. He couldn't remember a time when he'd slept so peacefully.

"Tony?"

"Mmm?"

"I've got to get up."

"Why?"

"Because Clem will be looking for his breakfast."

He opened one eye and peered at the clock. "Let him make his own."

"We can't just stay in bed all day," she pointed out.

"Sure we can."

"Don't you have things to do?"

"Oh, yes," he agreed, turning so that she was facing him. "This—" he said, giving her a leisurely, very thorough kiss "— and this—" he pulled her hips against his arousal "—and especially this." He stroked her inner thighs and moved upward to test her readiness for him. His actions made her sigh with unfeigned pleasure and she opened eagerly to him.

He joined them, careful not to rush her, but he needn't have worried. She was eagerly clutching him, moving with him with soft little moans that drove him wild.

He rolled to his back and arranged her legs on either side of his hips, then guided her into a rhythm they could both enjoy without ending their pleasure too soon.

He touched her breast with his tongue, then slipped his lips around the tip and tugged gently. "Oh, Tony," she whispered between panting breaths, "Oh . . . oh," she crooned in rhythm with him.

He couldn't control his responses much longer. He placed his hands on her hips and guided her with shorter, faster strokes until she let out a whimpering cry and stiffened, her body pulling him deeper, higher into her depths before he lost what little control he had.

Only then did he remember he'd forgotten to protect her from his early morning possession.

As soon as he thought his legs could hold his weight, he scooped her in his arms and strode from her bedroom into his, past the broken bed and into the bathroom. He switched on the shower, adjusted the water temperature, then allowed her to slowly slide down his body as the water washed over them.

He kept one arm around her waist while he industriously lathered first her back, then her front, taking special care to cover her breasts and to softly stroke between her legs. She leaned against the wall and smiled, holding out her hand. "My turn," she said.

Reluctantly he handed her the soap, knowing what the feel of her did to him. She carefully scrubbed his back, then his chest and downward, holding him gently as she soaped him all over.

"Christi?"

"Mmm."

"I forgot to protect you this morning."

Her long lashes veiled her eyes. "Oh."

"I'm sorry. I was more than half-asleep and I wasn't thinking about anything but—"

"It's okay."

"No. It's not okay."

"What I mean is that it's the wrong time for me to get pregnant."

"You're sure?"

She didn't look at him. She just nodded her head.

He lifted her chin so that those big green eyes had to meet his gaze. "Would you lie to me?"

Her gaze was shy but very steady. "No. You really have nothing to worry about. I promise."

Then she ducked her head under the water, dousing her curls. He grabbed the shampoo and began to run his hands through her hair, watching the foam and making little peaks on top of her head and over each ear before helping her rinse.

Once out of the shower, he helped her dry her hair and body before hastily finishing his own.

"I'll go start breakfast," she said.

"I'll be there shortly."

He watched her leave the bathroom, a towel wrapped around her, before he went about the business of shaving and dressing for his day.

They were both at the breakfast table when Clem came through the door.

"What in blazes happened?"

Tony stiffened, wondering how Clem could possibly know that he and Christina had... Then he remembered that Clem hadn't seen the kitchen since Christina added her touch to the room.

He grinned at the older man. "Livens the place up a bit, wouldn't you say?"

"Ducks?" Clem said, dazed.

"It was a choice between ducks, pigs and cows," he explained with a straight face.

"You mean you—"

"Christina decided to surprise me. She did all of this yesterday afternoon while I was working with you."

Clem looked around at the cabinets, the walls and the gaily patterned wallpaper.

"Do you like it?" she asked.

He poured himself some coffee and sat down before attempting to answer. He shifted his gaze to Tony, who smiled blandly.

"Looks real good," he said, nodding slowly. "Nice and bright." His quick glance took in the ruffled curtains before he buried his nose in his coffee cup.

They said very little over breakfast. Tony's thoughts kept returning to the hours he'd just spent with Christina, replaying in his mind how she'd felt and tasted.

"'He goeth after her straightway as an ox goeth to the slaughter.'"

Tony could feel his ears burning. He didn't look at either Christina or Clem.

"Where does that blasted bird git some of them silly sayings?" Clem asked, looking over at Minerva, who was preening her feathers in a wide arc.

"Mrs. Bledsoe taught her different Bible verses," Christina explained.

"I never heard anything about going like an ox to slaughter before."

"'Lust not after her beauty in thine heart,'" Minerva warned, causing Tony to squirm. He decided to change the subject.

"Do we have any lumber out in the barn to replace a broken bed slat?" he asked.

Clem's brows shot up in surprise as he glanced from Christina to Tony.

Oh, hell, Tony thought. He'd just made Clem think that . . . He closed his eyes in frustration at his predicament. It was then that Christina, bless her pure and innocent heart, blithely explained.

"It's my fault," she said, causing Clem's brows to climb almost to his hairline. "I forgot to tell Tony that Hercules is deathly afraid of thunderstorms."

"Thunderstorms?" the older man repeated, his puzzlement obvious.

"He's been that way since I first got him," she went on. "He's been sleeping in Tony's room since we arrived. Last night when the thunder started, he leaped up in the middle of the bed on top of Tony. The force of the jump caused the bed to collapse."

"Not to mention almost suffocating me with his weight," Tony added for good measure.

"Where's the dog now?" Clem asked, obviously convinced Tony had taken suitable measures, such as skinning him and hanging his hide on the barn door.

"Still asleep in the remains of my bed, obviously exhausted from the strain of his traumatic experience."

Clem coughed in a poor attempt to hide his amusement. "So where did you . . ." He realized that line of questioning was none of his business and quickly changed it to, "When do you want to fix the bed?"

Tony leaned back in his chair and stretched. "The sooner the better. I didn't get much sleep last night," he said with perfect truthfulness.

"I'll go look in the loft first thing," Clem replied, finishing his coffee. "Great breakfast, ma'am. If you keep this up, I'm going to be getting pretty hefty."

Christina waited until Clem had left before she looked at Tony and grinned. "You should be ashamed of yourself. 'I didn't get much sleep,'" she repeated, lowering her voice in imitation.

"Well, I didn't," he protested innocently.

"Maybe not. But how can you blame that on an innocent dog who's terrified of storms is beyond me."

He sighed. "I know. I'm past redemption," he admitted. "Which reminds me, Minerva's choice of quotes can be downright eerie at times. Do you coach her, by any chance?"

She laughed and shook her head. "Don't tell me you've been 'lusting after my beauty,'" she teased.

"You mean you haven't noticed? I've been wasting my time?"

She stacked the breakfast dishes, stood, leaned over and placed a hard kiss on his mouth. "On the contrary, you've been very instructive, and I want you to know I appreciate the lessons."

"Lessons?" He felt as though a cold hand had brushed down his spine.

"You know—lovemaking lessons. I had no idea that sex felt so good. No wonder people talk about it so much. It's really powerful. I'll never forget it." She picked up the dishes and walked over to the sink.

He stared at her back, feeling his anger grow. "Is that what you think's been happening here? A little sex education?"

She looked around with a surprised expression. "What is it? What did I say to upset you?"

He got to his feet and strode over to her. "You don't know? Do you think I just hop into bed with any woman who takes my fancy? You think I just sleep around, like some kind of cheap, some kind of..." Words failed him.

She was the picture of dismay. "Oh, no, Tony. I mean, well, yes, I do think you probably can have any woman who attracts you. I can't imagine a woman silly enough to turn you down. But that doesn't mean I think you're cheap, or promiscuous or..." She paused for a moment. "Is that what this is all about? You're afraid I won't respect you in the morning kind of thing?"

"Dammit!" He spun on his heel and headed for the bedroom. "I must be out of my mind!"

"Tony?" she called, but he kept on going until he reached his room. He slammed the door. Hercules lifted his head and blinked sleepily at his intrusion.

"Get out of my bed, you lazy excuse for a dog. Haven't you caused enough trouble?"

Hercules scrambled off the bed, trying to get his footing on the sloping surface, then lumbered over to where Tony stood with his hands on his hips. He licked one hand.

"And that's another thing," he shouted. "Don't you have enough sense not to be friendly with someone who's yelling at you, for Pete's sake? Get out of here!"

He jerked the door open and watched Hercules amble out of the room.

Tony slammed the door once again.

My God, I'm having a tantrum! he thought in disgust. *A door-slamming, yelling tantrum. If Prometheus was handy, I'd probably kick the cat...and roast the bird on a spit!*

He wrested the mattress and springs off the bed, propping them against the wall. He replaced the slat that had fallen and picked up the pieces of the other one.

What was the matter with him this morning? He was going from satiated pleasure to rip-roaring anger. His emotions were bouncing around like yo-yos gone berserk.

He'd always taken pride in having control over his emotions. He'd never let anything or anyone get too close to him, much preferring a solitary life-style devoid of complications.

Well, he certainly had more than his share of complications now. For all he knew, Christina could be pregnant! If she were, he would be at fault.

If she were, would she let him know?

If she were, would she raise his child without a father rather than ask for his help? Would he be perpetuating yet another generation of Callaways who caused pain for those they loved?

He didn't want to hurt Christina. He loved her.

The truth of his feelings caused his knees to buckle, and he sat down on a nearby chair with a thump. Why had he just realized how he felt about her? Hadn't his behavior toward her been a signal that something unusual was going on?

He wasn't a womanizer by any stretch of the imagination. In all honesty, he was shy with women. The more aggressive the woman, the more he withdrew. He wasn't comfortable with the obvious come-ons that he saw around the rodeo scene. He wasn't good at innuendos or flirting or coaxing a woman into the sack.

Was that why Christina's remarks had touched a nerve? Why he felt used and taken advantage of? He hadn't the experience necessary to take what had happened between them lightly. They had shared something so special, so right to him that he felt totally committed to her, while she casually offered him her thanks for the sex education.

He rubbed his furrowed brow, feeling helplessly confused.

The phone rang. He picked up the extension there in his bedroom. "H'lo?"

"Mr. Callaway?"

"Yes."

"John Malone. I'm afraid I have some bad news for you."

Tony stiffened. "What is it?"

"Someone in the bank got wind of our investigation and alerted our quarry. Two bank employees didn't show up to work this morning and at the present time can't be located. We aren't certain whether they were part of the operation or whether they discovered too much and have been taken out. Either way, we've got serious problems on our hands. My people want to bring Christina in now, today, to make certain she can't be touched. She is proving to be an invaluable source of information for us. If we know that, so does the other side. There's going to be an all-out effort on their part to make sure she doesn't talk."

"I'll take care of her," Tony said.

"I'm convinced you'll do your best," Malone agreed in a soothing voice. "I'm just not certain that—"

"Mr. Malone, you told me that you know my father."

"Well, yes, but I don't see—"

"My father is one of the most powerful men in this state, wouldn't you agree?"

"Probably, but—"

"He knows how to protect himself and his family."

"No doubt about that, but—"

"Christina's family, Mr. Malone. For all intents and purposes, she's a Callaway. They won't find her. I promise you that."

"Well..." Malone paused. When Tony said no more, Malone added, "You won't take any unnecessary risks, will you?"

"I'll do whatever I need to do to ensure her safety."

"Well, we'll be in touch. I'll have to check with the head of the department."

"You do that," Tony said and hung up.

He picked up a piece of paper on which he'd scribbled a phone number what felt like a lifetime ago, but which in linear time had only been two days. He punched out the numbers and waited, giving an extension number.

"Mom, sorry to keep bothering you like this," he said, when Allison answered.

"Tony, I don't care what you say, we are not cutting our vacation short to save you from an unexpected guest." She sounded very firm.

He laughed. "Glad to hear it. What I'm calling for is to speak with Dad. Is he around?"

"You want to speak to your father?"

She made no effort to hide her surprise at his request. He couldn't blame her for her reaction. So much had changed for him in such a short time that he was having difficulty recalling why his stiff-necked pride had kept him from appreciating the positive role his father had played in his life during these past fifteen years.

"Yeah, if he's there."

He heard her call to his father and felt a measure of relief that the man was available.

"Tony?" Cole said, sounding puzzled.

Tony's throat tightened as his father's voice came on the line. "Hi, Dad," he said hoarsely. "Good to hear you. How's the vacation going?"

There was a brief pause. In a cautious tone, Cole said, "About what you'd expect. The kids are running our legs off. I keep telling them I'm too old for all this hoopla, but they won't listen."

"You aren't old, Dad. You'll never be old."

"Hah. Tell my feet that. We must have walked fifteen miles yesterday."

Tony could hear his mother's voice in the background and his dad's amused but muffled response. "Your mother said to tell you that she's making certain I bear up under all this strain by joining me in the hot tub each night and giving me a full-body massage."

Tony laughed. "No wonder you're feeling old. That kind of help can kill a man!"

Cole repeated his remarks to Allison, and he could hear them both laughing, the intimate sound of two happily married people. Tony felt a jolt of envy and a yearning to experience a similar relationship.

"Uh, Dad, I don't want to keep you, but—"

"No, problem, Son. I'm delighted you called."

"Dad, I need your help," Tony blurted out, knowing this was the first time in his life he'd spoken those words.

Eight

Cole Callaway looked ten years younger than his fifty-one years, despite the gray hair that only emphasized his dark good looks. He'd been the head of Callaway Enterprises for thirty-one years. The weight of his responsibilities may have bent him, but he'd never broken.

Tony should have known his dad would waste no time in dealing with the present situation.

Within hours of their conversation, Cole had arrived at the ranch to discuss what needed to be done.

He walked into the house through the kitchen and stopped cold, looking at the transformation. Damn, was everybody going to react that way? Tony wondered.

"Just sprucing the place up a bit," Tony explained nonchalantly. "How about some coffee?"

"Sounds good," Cole absently replied, looking all around the room. "This your idea?"

"Not exactly."

"Didn't think so."

"But I like it."

"Uh-huh."

"I want you to meet Christina."

Cole gave another quick look around. "So do I."

Tony stepped into the hallway. "Christina? My dad's here." He watched as she came out of her bedroom.

"I don't want to disturb the two of you," she explained, coming toward him. She wore jeans, a sleeveless top that showed her slim midriff, and sandals.

"He wants to meet you. This meeting is about you, remember."

She touched her hair in a nervous gesture. It had dried in its natural state after their shared shower that morning. "You look fine," he offered reassuringly.

The look she gave him was unreadable. "He's not here to see what I look like."

That's what you think, he thought.

He took her hand and led her back into the kitchen just in time to hear Minerva announce in an excited voice, "'O Lord, save me! Protect thy turtledove from the hawk!'"

Cole spun around and looked toward the source of the sound, then glanced at his son in disbelief. "Did that black bird just say what it sounded like it said?"

Tony grinned and spoke to the bird. "You're not any turtledove, loudmouth, so cool it."

"'Who will protect me from the wicked? Who will be my shield?'"

Cole walked over to the cage and peered inside. "How did you teach it to talk?"

Christina released Tony's hand and approached Minerva's cage in turn. "I'm afraid I can't take credit. She belonged to a neighbor of mine who thought talking birds should be taught more than sailors' oaths."

"Amazing," Cole replied, shaking his head.

"We also have a very friendly Great Dane and a bashful three-legged cat lurking around here somewhere."

Cole straightened and cocked an eye at Tony. *"We?"* he repeated softly.

Tony could feel his ears burn.

"They're mine, actually," Christina said with a smile. She stuck out her hand. "I'm Christina O'Reilly. You must be Allison's husband."

Cole grasped her hand and stared intently at her. "That I am. I'm very pleased to meet you, Ms. O'Reilly. I understand you and Allison are related."

"Not really," Tony insisted. "It's a very distant connection."

"I see," Cole said, obviously amused. Tony had no doubt that his dad *did* understand. He knew he wasn't being subtle about his feelings for Christina.

Tony poured Cole some coffee and the three of them sat down at the table.

"I thought about what you told me on the flight over here," Cole began, "and I think the simplest solution is for Christina to stay at the Circle C until she's needed to testify. The place is built like a fortress. There's no way anyone could sneak up on the place without being spotted. With that in mind, I called

Cody as soon as we landed to see what he thought about the plan. He agreed with me."

"I can take care of her," Tony began. "I just thought that—"

"Of course you can," Cole agreed. "That's what I told Cody. That you would be there to make sure she's all right."

He eyed his dad thoughtfully. "You think I should go with her?"

"Absolutely. She'll need you there," Cole promptly replied.

"Oh, but I don't want to take you away from the ranch and your rodeo commitments," Christina said. "I appreciate your concern—everybody's concern," she added, including Cole. "I'm just sorry that you had to get mixed up in all of this. I had no idea that my job in Atlanta would have such far-reaching consequences."

"You're more important than the ranch or my rodeo schedule," Tony said, not caring that he had given his feelings for Christina away to his dad. Cole's eyes narrowed slightly, but he didn't comment. Tony reached for Christina's hand. "Besides, you'll enjoy getting to know Cody and his wife Carina. They've got a houseful of kids that will love our menagerie, although Minerva may learn some phrases that have never been heard in church."

"Is this what you want to do?" Cole asked Tony. There was no doubt in either man's mind what he was asking.

"Absolutely." Tony held his father's gaze. "I'll have Clem move into the house and take care of things here, maybe hire a couple of men to help him in case the search for Christina actually gets this far."

"I've got the men, don't worry. They're already on the payroll. I intend to have a few of them stay at the Circle C to watch for any unusual traffic around there as well."

"Mr. Malone didn't know exactly when I'd be needed to testify," Christina said worriedly. "I can't take advantage of your hospitality indefinitely."

Cole patted her hand. "Of course you can. You're family now," he said with a welcoming smile. "Isn't that right, Tony?"

"Absolutely."

The back door opened and Clem walked in carrying a long board. "Hello, Cole. Didn't know you were in these parts," he said, grinning. He stuck out his hand. "Good to see you."

Cole stood and grabbed the proffered hand. "Thanks, Clem. You're looking fit."

"Yep, but this danged boy of yours keeps me hoppin', that's for sure." He turned to Tony. "Here's that new slat for your bed. Next time don't be so rough with it. It wasn't made for all that leapin' around."

Tony jumped up and grabbed the slat from Clem. "You're a real help, Clem," he said through gritted teeth. "I'll go put it in place right now." He spun around and headed out of the kitchen.

He heard a chair scrape behind him and Cole said, "You may want some help."

Just what I need, Tony thought, stifling an audible groan.

He was replacing the slat in the frame when he heard the bedroom door close behind him. When he straightened, he saw Cole leaning against the door, watching him.

"It was the dog, Dad," he explained. "The damn dog is afraid of thunder and we had a storm here last night. He leaped up on the bed and the slat broke. It's no big deal. Really."

Cole crossed his arms and leaned against the door, crossing his ankles as well.

"You're saying you haven't slept with her?" His gaze was steady, his tone mild.

"Well," he motioned toward the bed, "the collapsed bed is all perfectly innocent—"

"I understand that. That wasn't my question."

"Dad, I'm thirty years old, not some teenager sowing wild oats. It's really none of your business what I'm doing or not doing."

Cole leaned his head against the door and sighed. "I know that. Hell, you were grown by the time I first laid eyes on you. I'm just concerned about you, that's all. According to your mother, you only met this woman a few days ago and from what I recall, you weren't all that pleased to have her here."

"A lot has happened since then," Tony said.

"For example?"

"I mean, I've gotten to know her better. I understand her . . . and admire her. She's got a lot of courage. She's been on her own most of her life, but she hasn't let it stop her from enjoying life."

"In this day and age, a person can't be too discriminating," Cole said, picking his words with care. "You don't know enough about her to know whether—"

"She was a virgin," Tony blurted out.

"Was?"

"All right, so maybe I did rush things along, but I know how I feel." He paused, gathering his thoughts. "What I mean is, I know how you must have felt . . .

about Mom. It's like I found the other half of myself that I didn't know was missing until I met her. She's got my emotions going in all directions. I don't want to think about not having a life with her."

"Does she know how you feel?"

"I don't think so."

"Do you know how she feels?"

"About me?"

"About any of this."

He remembered her casual comments, which had stabbed him to his soul. "I don't think she has a clue. She's got some weird idea that men don't find her attractive, that she'll be single all her life, which doesn't seem to bother her."

"I don't know how to break the news to you, Son," Cole drawled, "but today's women have discovered that they can have perfectly comfortable, productive, well-rounded lives without having a man about."

Tony frowned. "Are you making fun of me?"

"Not at all. I'm just saying that it isn't a foregone conclusion a woman will automatically decide that marriage is her destiny. You should hear your sister go on about the subject. It's highly enlightening."

"I love her, Dad."

Cole straightened away from the door and walked over to his son. He hugged him, then slapped him on the back. "I'd say that's a good first step. Why don't you gather what you need for a few weeks and take her down to the Circle C? Spend some time with her, get to know her a little more. Once you're certain that your feelings haven't changed, then tell her what's in your heart."

"What if she doesn't care?" Tony had a tough time getting the words out.

"You'll have to accept whatever happens. We don't really have much control over how another person feels. I learned that lesson fairly fast where you're concerned."

"What do you mean?"

"I mean that I know you've wrestled with how you relate to me and to the Callaway clan. I was proud that you were willing to take my name, but that's about all you've ever accepted from me. I'm here to tell you that when I hung up that phone from talking with you this morning, I bawled like a baby. I've been waiting for you to ask for something from me for a long, long time."

Tony's eyes filled. "I love you, Dad."

"I know. That's what got me through all of this."

"And I really appreciate your dropping everything and coming over like you have."

Cole smiled. "Having a private plane at my disposal eases things along. Tom's waiting in Austin to get me back over there by the time the family's finished their day's exploration. Your mom thinks I put you up to calling just to give me a day's rest."

"You can show her how much you benefited from the rest by giving *her* one of those full-body massages."

Cole laughed. "Yep, those massages have got quite a family history."

Tony had a sudden flash of the night before, with Christina kneeling beside him, her hands and lips kissing and exploring him. He flushed. "I'll have to try one sometime," he managed to say.

"Here, let me help you with this box spring and mattress. I suppose Clem will be staying in here while you're gone."

"Yeah. I want him close to the phone. I'll have him notify me if anything happens around here that's in the least suspicious."

Four hands and two strong backs made short work of the bed. When the two men left the room, more than a bed had been restored to a better condition.

When Christina decided to visit Texas and look up the names on her family tree, she'd had no idea that Allison Alvarez had married into one of the richest, most powerful families in Texas.

Granted, she'd been impressed with the home she'd visited in Austin and had decided that Cole Callaway must be a successful businessman. Tony's ranch had shown signs of care and industry, and the buildings were in good repair, but there was nothing fancy about the place. He'd mentioned going to the bank for a possible loan, like everyone else she knew.

Only now was she beginning to understand the wealth of the Callaways. Cole had flown from Florida to Texas in a private jet. The Callaway companies owned several planes. The house she had seen in Austin was only one of several. The ranch they were presently heading to had been in the family for four generations. Earlier, Tony had explained that his uncle Cody lived there and the other two brothers—Cole and Cameron—visited whenever they had the time. Their visits never inconvenienced anyone because each brother had his own wing in the hacienda-style Big House, as Tony called it.

His own wing? She'd heard about the state that liked to brag about everything being bigger and better, but she'd never expected to witness the phenomena with her own eyes.

One thing she knew without doubt, though—the Callaways were much too rich for her orphan blood. Of course, she'd always known that at most she could have only a casual sort of relationship with Tony. She'd never considered for a moment having anything else. Wishes and dreams could only stretch so far, and Tony was way beyond her wildest dream.

But, oh! She would never forget him, not for as long as she lived. She had learned years ago to live in the moment, to accept what happened each day as though she were being given a gift to enjoy. She refused to make herself miserable by creating unrealistic expectations that could never materialize.

She wondered if there was a possibility that she might be pregnant. She hadn't wanted to let herself think about it for fear of disappointment. A baby... Tony's baby. To have something that was a part of him would be the greatest gift life could offer her.

What she'd told him was the truth. She wasn't supposed to get pregnant at this stage of her cycle. Hoping she was wrong was one more expectation that was counterproductive.

"Do you want to stop somewhere to eat?"

Tony's question pulled her attention back to the van and their trip south. Because of the animals, they had decided to travel in her vehicle, where there was more room. She glanced at Hercules stretched out on his special blanket, Prometheus curled up on his pillow and Minerva's covered cage.

"That would be nice," she said, smiling at the man driving.

"We need gas, anyway."

They hadn't had much to say to each other since Cole left the ranch. Tony had explained their plans to Clem, she had packed her things, Tony had thrown some clothes in a suitcase, they had gathered the pets into the van and left the T Bar C Ranch behind them.

Tony had appeared preoccupied, which wasn't surprising. She had come for a quick visit and ended up completely rearranging his life. They hadn't said much to each other since he'd stormed out of the kitchen right after breakfast. She'd had time to replay their conversation several times in her mind during the day and she was still confused over his reaction.

Tony turned off the interstate on the outskirts of San Antonio and pulled into a gas station. After filling the tank, he drove into the parking lot of a chain restaurant next door.

"Will they be all right?" he asked, locking the van and peering through the window.

"Yes. That's why I have bars on the back windows—so I can leave them open when I have to stop. They're used to traveling by now. I spent my weekends exploring the southeastern part of the country when I worked. I just packed them up and took them with me."

They went inside and sat down. After giving the waitress their order, Christina said, "I was wondering if I could ask you something."

Tony leaned back in his chair. He didn't like the serious tone of her voice. "Ask away."

"I recognize that I'm naive about male-female relationships, and that I'm showing my ignorance, but I really want to know something."

"I'll be happy to answer any question you have."

"Why were you so angry this morning?"

She watched him closely, trying to read his expression, but he was good at hiding what he was thinking.

"Lack of sleep, maybe?" he replied with a lop-sided smile.

"You acted as if I'd insulted you. I certainly didn't mean to, and I'm sorry if I said something to make you think that."

He sighed. "I'm sorry for blowing up like that," he admitted. "It was stupid to throw a tantrum because I felt misunderstood. I guess I'm not handling this situation very well."

"What situation?"

"The way I feel about you."

Christina's heart began to pound in her chest. What was he saying? She stared at him, nonplussed. He reached over and took her hand.

"I don't want to rush you," he went on. "The last thing I want is to scare you off. I want to give us some time together, to get to know each other. That's why I'm coming to the ranch with you. Dad was teasing me about your needing me there. You'd do just fine. Carina's wonderful. She'd make you feel at home right away. Cody will make certain the place is safe. He's tough, with a lot of experience. I just didn't like the idea of not seeing you."

She didn't want to start believing in something that wasn't there, that wouldn't happen. That way lay pain and heartache.

"Is it because we made love?"

His brows drew together in confusion. "What do you mean?"

"Do you think you're obligated to look after me because we went to bed together?"

"No, of course not."

"Then I guess I still don't understand why you're saying this, why you're taking time away from your ranch to be with me."

He closed his eyes for a moment, showing frustration. "You don't have a clue, do you?" he said after a moment. When she didn't answer, he took a deep breath.

"Christina, have you ever loved anybody?"

"No." She didn't have to think about that one.

"Not anyone at all?"

"I have warm feelings for Mrs. Bledsoe...and of course, my pets."

"Not anyone else, like someone you've dated?"

She laughed. "No."

He hesitated, as though wanting to say more, then shook his head. "Let's just take this one step at a time, okay? Let's go to the ranch, hang out for whatever length of time we need to keep you safe before you have to testify, and get to know each other. I want to be your friend, Christina. I want you to learn to trust me, to come to rely on me."

"I do trust you, and what is this trip if it isn't an example of my relying on you?"

"But you don't need me."

"Well, no, that's true."

"You could have gone with John Malone, to be kept in protective custody somewhere."

"Yes, although I may have had some difficulty because of my pets."

"Oh, I'm quite sure of that!"

"You've accepted them all right," she pointed out.

"Yeah, well, I must admit that surprises me, but you're right. I've gotten used to having them around...even self-righteous Minerva."

The meals arrived and they spoke little until they were back in the van, heading south once more.

"Have you ever wanted to need someone?" Tony asked several miles down the road.

What a strange question, she thought. Maybe he was trying to make conversation to keep her from getting bored. "I don't think so," she replied. "I've never pictured myself as a helpless person."

"You don't have to be helpless in order to need other people in your life to make it complete. As a matter of fact, I just recently learned that lesson myself. I thought I had to stay totally independent of my family to prove I could make it without them. I learned I was wrong. It's not a sign of weakness to admit I need other people."

"Is that why you told your dad before he left that you'd like his help buying rodeo stock?"

Tony grinned. "Yeah. You would have thought I'd given him a priceless gift, when I was actually hitting him up for a loan."

"I'm sure he can afford it."

"I guess that's one of the reasons I've been so prickly about wanting to take anything from him. Sounds a little silly, now that I'm talking about it."

"You love your family very much. It shows whenever you talk about them."

"They could become your family, too, if you wanted them to be."

She rested her head on the seat, considering his remarks. "What a lovely idea. I could be an honorary member of the Callaway clan, a part of the family." She looked at him as he concentrated on the road. "I wonder what the rest of the family would think?"

"They'd accept you with open arms, believe me."

"It's certainly something to think about, I must admit."

Once again they lapsed into silence. Christina was glad that Tony was driving, so that she could watch the ever-changing landscape. When he began to slow down, she saw a pair of adobe pillars supporting an arched wrought-iron sign with a large *C* in a circle.

"We're here!" she said, feeling a sense of anticipation.

"Close, but not there."

"Isn't that the gate?" she asked, pointing over her shoulder. It was fancier than the one at Tony's, but it gave the same sense of being on ranch property.

"Oh, yes. But we still have a ways to go."

So she found out. After several miles they reached the top of an incline, and Tony stopped the van so she could see this first view of the Circle C Ranch.

She caught her breath in amazement. It looked like a village. Nestled in the hills was a rambling, multi-storied stucco building with a Spanish-tiled roof. A wall encircled the cluster of buildings, with an arched opening in it for the road.

"Oh, Tony, it's beautiful! I had no idea. It looks as though we've traveled back in time a hundred years."

"Be thankful we haven't. The family keeps the place up-to-date. There's running water, indoor toilets, all the comforts of modern-day life."

She turned to him, unable to contain her excitement. "This is where I'll be staying?"

"Where *we'll* be staying!" he corrected.

"How do you keep from getting lost in a place that size?"

"The main part of the house is laid out very simply around a courtyard. Most of the rooms on the first floor open onto the courtyard, so you can't get too confused.

"Upstairs the hallway splits off in three directions. We'll be using dad's wing. He and Mom seldom come down. Even if they do, there're several bedrooms in each wing."

"Do you have any idea how lucky you are to be a part of all of this?"

"Yeah. Finally, I think I'm beginning to understand how fortunate I am. You see, until I was fifteen, I thought my mother was the only relative I had in the world. I remember what that felt like. I can relate to what you've gone through. Now I want to share my family with you. We'll learn to appreciate them together."

Nine

"So you're flying to Washington tomorrow, are you?" Cody said to Tony. They'd decided to escape the hacienda for a few hours and ride into the hills.

"That's right. Dad and I are escorting Christina in the jet. We'll be staying with her for however long it takes for her to testify."

"I'm going to miss having y'all here. Christina's been great company for Carina. She's got my girls with rainbow-colored toenails, taught Carina how to make some unusual crafts. Hell, I'm even going to miss that damn bird preaching at me."

"It was your idea to put Minerva in the solarium. I would have kept her upstairs, you know."

Cody grinned. "Yeah, but then I couldn't have taught her a few phrases of my own without Christina catching me."

"I warned her that you'd corrupt that bird."

"Who, me?"

"You don't mind looking after Hercules?"

Cody adjusted his hat and shook his head. "I've never known a dog like him. He lets the kids ride on his back or sprawl all over him, lets the baby pull his ears without a whimper...yet sets the place on edge with his howls when it storms."

"I'll admit he's not your run-of-the-mill canine."

"How about you? What are your plans after all this is over?"

"That depends."

"On what?"

"If Christina agrees to marry me."

Cody lifted his brow slightly. "You mean there's a chance she won't?"

"I don't know. I keep putting off asking her."

"No lie! Afraid of what she'll say?"

"Something like that."

"Well, don't look to me for advice. I fell into marriage backwards and upside down. It took me a few years to get it all straightened out to my satisfaction."

"You have a great marriage, Cody."

"'Course I do. That's because of Carina. That woman managed to whip me into shape, cured me of my wild and woolly ways, keeps me home and makes me love it."

"I never gave marriage a thought until I met Christina. It took me less than forty-eight hours to realize that she was the only woman I'd ever love."

"You've known her how long?"

"We'd just met a few days before we came here. We've been here—" he thought for a moment "—almost three months. At least she has. I've had to go back to my place every week or so."

"Has she made any plans for when the trial is over?"

"She's still paying rent on a place in Atlanta. Seems she thinks she's supposed to go back there and find a job. I keep telling her she's not going to be able to do anything like that after testifying in this case."

"So you're going to offer an alternative?"

Tony nodded, a slight smile hovering on his lips. "I guess I can't accuse her of burying her head in the sand, since that's what I've been doing all these years."

"What are you talking about?"

"Dad finally told me that, like every other member of this family, I draw a percentage of the profits of Callaway Enterprises on a quarterly basis. But when I got touchy about his paying for my college fees, he decided not to mention that he'd set up an account for me as soon as he knew I existed. It's just been sitting there for all these years, untouched, adding interest and compounding interest. He took a certain amount of it and invested it in a few stocks and other things." Tony rubbed his neck. "Here I've been watching my pennies, determined to make it on my own, while I had all that money waiting for me."

"Cole's no fool, Tony. He knew what you were going through."

"Well, I guess meeting Christina opened my eyes to lots of things. I'm here to tell you that it makes my life much simpler to offer to place her in my own witness-protection program. She'll become Christina Callaway of the Texas Callaways. The Feds are fairly certain no one on the other side knows where she is. They think she went into hiding, and they don't know the government agents found her. Once she's testified, we're going to whisk her out of there without a trace and quietly erase all sign of her in Atlanta. Dad has the contacts to do it without anyone knowing how it was done. We'll come back here until she and I decide, together, where we'll live and what we'll do."

"You still want to ranch?"

"Oh, yeah. If she wants to stay where I am, we can do that. I want to build us another place. We'll let Clem have the house. I want Christina to create the kind of home she wants."

"Doesn't that scare you a little? I mean, that woman does get carried away with color schemes from time to time."

"I can live with it."

"So. Everything's set with just one minor detail. You don't have Christina's agreement to the whole idea."

"I don't want her to feel that she has to marry me in order to be safe. Dad made me promise not to try to force her into marriage. He said that, if she truly prefers to remain single, he'll have a long talk with her, explain the government's concern, maybe even convince her the government is footing the bill—which they would do, by the way—and help her start over somewhere else. At least I've got her becoming comfortable with the idea she's part of the Callaway clan."

"You just want to make it legal, is that it?"

"You got it."

"I don't envy you your selling job. She strikes me as a woman who's comfortable with her independence."

"That's why I've spent the past three months letting her see that having me in her life wouldn't take away from her independence. I just want to be a part of her life."

"My, how the mighty have fallen. I can't believe I'm hearing this from Tony Mr. Independence Himself Callaway. Anyway, I wish you the best of luck. If I can help in any way, I hope you'll let me know."

"You've already helped tremendously by letting her see a happy marriage, a contented family circle and the normal workings of a household. It's amazing what she didn't have in the way of social and family interaction when she was growing up. I've noticed in the last few weeks that she's stopped watching from the sidelines and begun to take part in the family gatherings."

Cody glanced at the sun, which was hovering over the western hills. "Guess it's time we head back. Thanks for keeping me company this afternoon. Riding out like this soothes me, somehow. It helps me keep my perspective on life. When I was kid I could hardly wait to leave home. I knew I was an adult when I could hardly wait to come back."

"I know the feeling exactly," Tony said as they turned their horses back toward home.

Christina watched the two riders in the hills, silhouetted by the setting sun, draw closer to the house. Tony would soon be home.

She felt so silly, getting excited every time she saw him, as though they'd been separated for days. Since they'd moved to the Circle C, he'd never been gone longer than a day and a night, when he went to check on his place.

She'd never admitted to him how much she wished she could go with him on his trips, because she knew she had to stay hidden here until after the trial.

She had such mixed feelings about the upcoming ordeal. On one hand she was eager to have it behind her, feeling as though there were a sword dangling over her neck while she waited. On the other hand she knew that once the trial was over there would be no more need for her to hide, and therefore no more need to stay with Tony.

Need was such a strange sensation. She remembered a conversation she's had with Tony a few months ago. He'd asked something to the effect of whether she ever wanted to need someone. She'd thought the question strange at the time. She didn't know about *wanting* to experience such a thing, but she had certainly discovered all about *needing* someone.

If she wanted to get fanciful, she'd discovered a whole list of needs she'd never thought of before, like the need to wake up and find Tony asleep beside her, his hair rumpled, his face unshaven . . . the need to reach out and touch him at night to make certain she hadn't dreamed up his existence . . . the need to hold him and feel his desire for her pressing against her, making her feel seductive and desirable and wanted . . . the need to look up from whatever she was doing and see him watching her with a soft smile. . . the need to fall asleep every night with his arms around her, knowing she was safe from the world.

Yes, she had come to understand about need. It had made her feel more vulnerable than she'd ever felt before. It made her want more than she could have, yearn for the glitter of a far-off star. It made her want to believe in the magic of a special world where all her dreams would come true.

She had to keep reminding herself to just enjoy the moment. She had today. If she enjoyed each minute, appreciated every happening, no matter how small, she would have a wonderful collection of memories that no one could take away from her.

The riders reached the barn. She watched them climb off the horses and turn them over to trainers who would see to their needs. The men walked toward the house, talking intently, their heads close together.

She'd been surprised at how much Tony and Cody resembled each other. They could easily have passed for brothers. Tony rubbed his rump and laughed, pretended to take a couple of limping steps before continuing toward the side door in his normal gait.

She spun away from the window and hurried to the bathroom, one of her favorite places in the house. The walls were lined with mirrors and there was a large hot tub where she and Tony had spent some highly charged moments.

She really was without shame where he was concerned. She had learned so much about lovemaking in general and how to please him in particular. He'd taught her about her own sensual nature.

She quickly adjusted the taps and dumped in a few ingredients to scent the water and soften it. Then she pulled her blouse over her head and unfastened her jeans.

"Christina? Where are you?" Tony called, coming down the hallway.

Her first day here, he had shown her to a bedroom that opened onto this bathroom. With a wicked grin, he'd opened another door and shown her the master bedroom. If she went to bed in her own room at night, he joined her. Other times he coaxed her into sharing his. No one knew that they slept together in the privacy of the suite, and if one of the maids may have mentioned it, nothing was ever said.

Cody and Carina accepted her so completely that she felt as though she warmed herself with their friendly openness much like she might warm her hands near a friendly fire.

She heard the door to the master bedroom open. "Christina? You in here?"

She grabbed a towel and wrapped it around her. "I'm here," she said a little shyly, stepping out of the bathroom.

He spun toward her at the sound of her voice, then did a slow and penetrating visual inspection from her bare toes to her hair pinned on top of her head.

"Am I interrupting something?" he drawled, reaching for the snaps of his western shirt.

"Not at all. I'm just getting ready to go into the hot tub and was hoping you'd join me."

"You saw me coming?"

"Uh-huh. I saw you and Cody ride in. I thought a relaxing soak might ease some of those weary muscles before dinner."

He tossed the shirt to the side, hopped a couple of steps jerking off his boots, unzipped his jeans and stepped out of them and ended up in front of her, a trail of clothes marking his route.

He casually took her towel and flipped it over his shoulder, then picked her up by crossing his arms beneath her rump and lifting her so that her breasts were pressed against his face. "I've missed you," he mumbled, nuzzling and nipping her, teasing the tips with his tongue, then giving a sharp, erotic pull on them.

There must be a direct connection between her breasts and her lower body, Christina decided, because every time he touched her, she became moist and eager for him.

He ambled into the bathroom without looking, still kissing and caressing her, making her tremble with anticipation. By the time he allowed her to slide down his body, he was pulsatingly hard.

She made no effort to stiffen her knees, but allowed herself to kneel and take him into her mouth, teasing him in the same way he had teased her, with the nibbling, sucking bites that made her wild.

Funny how he seemed to have the same reaction.

She loved to hear him groan with helpless pleasure. She loved the way he gripped her head, running his long fingers through her hair.

"Enough," he finally said, stepping back from her, making no attempt to hide his trembling. "You're going to unman me!"

"Oh, I don't think so," she replied, rubbing her hands up, down and all around his solid length. She moved away and stepped into the tub, turning off the tap. Sinking down into the water, she looked up at him impishly and said, "Care to join me?"

She barely got the words out of her mouth when he was climbing in beside her, sliding down and reaching for her at the same time. He tugged her to him, urgently pulling her knees wide and around his hips. With a feverishness she'd rarely seen in him since she'd known him, he adjusted their positions and slid his length deep inside, clutching her to him and holding her tightly as he began a furious rhythm that swept her away.

The water quickly became choppy with waves as she hooked her feet behind him and held on, giving him long, moist kisses and teasing him with her thrusting tongue.

He stiffened, dropped his head back and let out a shout. She felt the same convulsive surges from her core and could only hang on to him, helpless to combat the wave after wave of intense pleasure that swept through her.

She lost track of how long they stayed in that same position. It didn't matter. Tony had never been like this before—so out of control. They had made love in the tub before, but only the preliminaries. They had always ended in bed, where he...

Where he always carefully used protection.

But not this evening.

This time she wasn't in the safe part of her cycle. This time she could very easily become pregnant.

She rested her head on his shoulder. There was little she could do at this point. She would just have to deal with the consequences of their behavior when and if it became necessary.

Dinnertime at the Callaways was always a laughing, noisy affair. All four of Cody's children ate with their parents, including the baby, ten-month-old Denise.

Christina spent her time helping Carina feed Denise, who sat in her high chair between Carina on the end and Christina to her right.

The men talked about cattle and raising horses, while answering the hundred-and-one questions asked by Clay, Sherry and Kerry.

Once in a while Tony would casually place his hand on Christina's thigh and stroke it lightly from her knee to her hip. When she'd look at him, he would give her the innocent smile of a choirboy.

After dinner Carina took Denise upstairs to get her ready for bed. Cody suggested that once the kids were down, the four of them could play spades. Christina was surprised to hear Tony say, "Not tonight, Cody. Christina and I have some things to discuss before our trip tomorrow."

Cody winked and said, "Sure, I understand. I guess we'll see you tomorrow before you leave, then."

Tony slipped his fingers between hers and led her up the stairs and down the long hallway to his bedroom. Once inside, he adjusted the light before leading her over to the love seat in front of the TV.

He sat down and pulled her into his lap. She laughed. "Do you realize that you never let me sit on a piece of furniture? I always end up in your lap. I'm surprised you don't sit that way in the dining room."

"The thought has crossed my mind a few times, I must admit."

"And what was this stroking-my-thigh business to-night? You would have been awfully shocked if I'd reached over and grabbed you in a sensitive area."

"Not at all," he replied with dignity. "I would have politely excused us from the table and brought you upstairs to finish what you'd started."

"You're insatiable, you know that?"

"It's your fault. You've trained me very well. This is a perfect example of the student surpassing the teacher."

She kissed him on the nose. "You're so silly."

"Not tonight. Tonight I'm serious. I need to talk to you. It's very difficult for me to talk to you because I get distracted and forget what I was trying to say. I keep touching you and one thing leads to another, and before I know it I'm completely inert, immobilized and brain dead. Therefore, I refuse to allow you to have your way with me . . . at least not until I've said what I mean to say."

She folded her hands together in a demure pose. "What is it you have to say?"

She waited for him to begin. He cleared his throat, made a couple of sounds that faintly resembled words though she wouldn't swear to it, then said, "About tomorrow." His voice sounded hoarse.

"What about tomorrow?"

"We're going to DC."

"We discussed that three weeks ago. Have the plans changed?"

"Uh, no. You're to testify, then we fly back here."

She nodded. "Okay."

"What we haven't discussed is the fact that once you testify, you will be marked by the people who are on trial."

"According to the prosecutor, my testimony will guarantee them very long prison sentences."

"That doesn't mean they can't see to it that you pay for putting them there."

"Well, the first night they interviewed me, Mr. Malone did discuss the possibility that I might have to go into a witness-protection program."

"He did?"

"Yes."

"You never mentioned it to me."

"I didn't think it had anything to do with you."

"Do you still feel that way?"

Puzzled by his line of questioning, she asked, "Well, since we're talking about my job at the bank, my discovery of the accounts, my testimony regarding them and my possible danger as a result, I'd say yes. This is about me, not you."

"Do you always have to be so blasted logical?"

She drew back. "My logic makes you angry?"

"Frustrated. Very frustrated."

"That happens a lot when you talk with me. Do you suppose we have a problem communicating?"

"Only in some areas," he said, slipping his hand into the collar of her shirt and cupping her bare breast. "Other times I notice you get my message just fine."

"I always get your messages, Tony."

"Are you sure?"

She watched him for a moment, trying to figure out his mood. "I think so."

"All right. Let's test your little theory. Are you aware that I'm in love with you?"

She caught her breath. "In love?" she repeated faintly.

"Yes. Not to be confused with in like or fond of or merely interested in, but the whole nine yards. I am besotted with you, dream about you, can't stop thinking about you, in love with you. There. Did that get my message across plainly enough?"

She was shaking inside. She couldn't help it. She was hearing Tony say things she'd never thought to hear, never expected to hear. She wanted to laugh and cry at the same time. Instead, she laid her forehead on his shoulder and said, "Oh, Tony."

"That wasn't the response I was hoping to hear." He sounded rueful.

"Wh-what do you want to hear?"

"How you feel about me."

"Oh." She smiled. "That's easy. I love you."

"Just like that?"

"Uh-huh."

"You told me you'd never loved anybody before."

"I never have."

"But you just said—"

"Except you."

He seemed to relax a little. "So. You really do love me," he mused. "That gives me hope."

"For what?"

"That you'll marry me."

She felt like he'd slapped her. She scrambled off his lap and backed away from him, arms outstretched as though to ward him off. "I've never known you to be cruel before, Tony. Please don't joke about something like that."

"My God, woman, you think I'm joking?" He, too, leaped off the couch and glared at her. "What did you think I was doing, living here with you for the past three months, just killing time until the trial?"

"No, of course not. You obviously enjoy my company. We have fun, but we've neither one talked about the possibility of a future together."

"Only because I thought you'd take off running at the mention of the idea."

"Tony, let's be sensible about this. I can't tell you how wonderful it is to know that you love me. It explains so much—your patience with me . . . your kindness and understanding. I couldn't get over how—''

"Just call me Saint Tony," he offered sarcastically.

"All I'm saying is that it makes sense to me that you've acted out of loving feelings for me. I know I've loved you for a long time. At first I didn't understand what it was I was feeling. I mean, how could I? I thought love was what I felt for Mrs. Bledsoe!"

"I know!"

"Well, I certainly feel differently toward you than I do her."

"Glad to hear it," he said dryly.

"But marriage is something else again."

"Oh, I don't know. Generally it's all part of the whole. You fall in love with someone, then you court them—or in my case, try to get you to fall in love with me. Then you marry them. It's really a relatively simple process."

"But I've never thought about getting married!" she wailed.

"Oh, I can believe that easily enough. Why do you think we're having this particular conversation tonight?"

"Why?"

"So you can think about it."

"You mean, actually think about the possibility of you and me getting married?"

"Does the concept totally boggle your mind? It sounds really natural to me."

She stood on one side of the room while he stood on the other. She didn't want him to come any closer. She didn't want her reason to be compromised by the feelings he always evoked every time he came close to her.

"It's because you think I might be pregnant, isn't it?"

"What? When? How could—?"

"Tonight when we were in the hot tub."

He smacked his palm against his forehead. "I can't believe I never gave it a thought." He lowered his hand slowly. "Yes, I can. I've been thinking of you as my wife for so long that I don't really care if you get pregnant or not. I want a family. I want to look just like Cody and Carina in a few years, with a dining table lined up with our little ones."

"You're shouting," she said quietly.

"Then it's a good thing Minerva's downstairs, or she'd be lecturing me right now!"

Christina grabbed her mouth but the giggle escaped. He gave her a ferocious frown.

"You're yelling at me because you want to marry me and have a family," she pointed out.

"No, I'm not. I'm yelling because you can't believe that I want to marry you."

"But if I go into the witness-protection program—"

"Why do you think I'm discussing this with you now? If you agree to marry me, you won't need to go into their program. We have one already going for you here in Texas. Nobody knows who you are. We can make up a different past for you. Dad will erase all sign of you in Atlanta—retrieve your things, close up the house, that kind of thing. He knows what needs to be done."

His dad, she thought. Cole Callaway, of the Texas Callaways.

"I can't marry you, Tony," she said steadily. "I wish you hadn't asked me."

He looked as though he'd been struck by lightning. He stiffened and stared at her, his eyes wide with shock. "You can't?" he whispered hoarsely. "Why not?"

She had to swallow twice before she could answer. Why was he forcing her to put it into words? Why should she have to spell it out? "Because you're a Callaway, that's why," she said with dignity. Then she turned and walked through the bathroom to the other bedroom.

Ten

———

Tony sank back into the seat beside his father and strapped himself in. Christina had chosen to spend the flight in the small bedroom at the back of the plane, which was just fine with him. He had no more desire to see her than she did to see him.

He stared blindly out of the window as the runway raced by, then fell below them in a stomach-grabbing drop.

"Trouble in paradise?" Cole asked.

He fought a strong desire to lie. He didn't want to talk about what had happened to him. However, they had a long flight ahead of them. Tony knew his dad well enough to know he wouldn't ignore his silence for much longer. He shrugged after a long pause and muttered, "Something like that."

"Want to talk about it?"

"There's nothing to talk about."

"Meaning?"

"That when we get through in Washington, Christina O'Reilly intends to get on with her life and I intend to get on with mine."

"She turned you down, huh?"

"Flat."

"I see."

Tony continued to stare out the window.

"You're pretty angry about it, I take it."

"Yeah, I guess you could say that."

Tony thought his dad had decided to drop the subject, because nothing more was said for several minutes. Then Cole spoke again. "You know, the thing about anger is that it can create a smoke screen so we don't have to look at what we're *really* feeling."

Tony didn't reply. Instead, he closed his eyes and dropped his head on the back of the seat, feeling very vulnerable and exposed.

"I have a hunch you're hurting pretty badly about now."

"Yeah," Tony whispered.

"I remember like it was yesterday finding your mother after losing touch with her for over fifteen years." His dad's voice was low and Tony could hear the pain in it. "God, I had never stopped loving that woman. I felt like my heart had been ripped out of my chest when she disappeared."

Tony certainly knew that feeling. He'd had a gaping wound in his chest since the night before.

"Finding her...and you...again was the best thing that had happened to me. I immediately began to make plans. I was convinced that our lives would be worked out in a new and better way.''

Tony straightened, shifting in his chair. "I remember. You asked her to marry you and she said no." He'd forgotten about that.

"That's right."

He thought about that time in his own history, trying to put himself in his father's place. "Is this how you felt?"

Cole nodded. "I bet it's pretty damn close."

Tony looked at him, recognizing a fellow sufferer. "How did you survive the pain?" he asked quietly.

Cole shook his head slowly, as though reliving that time in his life. "I took a real nosedive. Wished I could die. Prayed for it. But then I remembered that I now had a son and that I could at least get to know him."

Tony nodded. "I remember how you used to call and talk with me." He smiled at the memory. "It felt good to have a real father. I was so proud of you. You were famous and everything."

"That's why your mother didn't want to marry me."

Startled, Tony asked, "Why? Because you were famous?"

"Because I was a Callaway."

Tony jerked forward in his seat. "That's exactly what Christina said! Can you believe it? What does that mean? Why would they both . . . It doesn't make sense. It just doesn't . . . make . . . sense!"

He leaned over and rested his head on the heels of his hands, his elbows propped on his knees.

Cole reached out and rubbed his son's back. He loved the man beside him so much, more than he could find words to express. He'd been deprived of so much with this child of his. Katie and the twins had given him another chance to enjoy a family, but they couldn't give him his firstborn's childhood. He'd grown to accept what he couldn't change because he had no choice.

To see Tony in so much pain almost brought him to his knees. Tony could get to him like none of the others. He was so proud. So independent. So aloof. Cole had been loving him from afar for a long time now. He blessed the young woman who'd come into his son's life because she had triggered so many things in him. She'd caused him to open up, to share his heart's desire with his father.

If there was any way on God's green earth he could, Cole wanted to provide his son with that heart's desire.

He continued to rub Tony's back and felt his shoulders heave, but there were no sounds.

"I was really puzzled by your mother's decision," he went on, as though there'd been no interruption. "It didn't make any sense to me. I guess that's why they say men are so different from women. I figured that I loved her and she loved me, so we'd naturally want to get married. Seemed simple enough."

Tony nodded, but kept his head in his hands.

He was listening.

"So I decided to give her some time to think about it. I insisted on keeping the lines of communication open between us. I remember getting pretty corny at times, telling her that I would wait for her forever if need be. Just because it was the truth didn't make it any less corny, you understand. I tried to draw her out, get her to explain her feelings. Of course, the Callaways had hurt her and her dad pretty bad, and she had reason to hold a grudge. The funny thing was she'd forgiven us for that. What she was having so much trouble with was the family name, the legends, the money, the power. Most people might think those things would make life a hell of a lot easier—and I'll admit that at times it does. At least it's damn convenient. But when it comes to matters of the heart, well, that seems to be a different story. It can also be seen as control. If there's one thing Allison didn't want, it was to lose control over her own life.''

Tony straightened and leaned back against the chair once again. His eyes, when he looked at Cole, were red but dry.

"Do you think that's the way Christina feels?"

"Could be. She's made her own way in the world for a while. As far as I can see, she's done a fine job of taking care of herself. It seems to me that you'd be able to understand that need. I remember you made it real clear to me that I couldn't buy you, that you didn't want or need my help, that just because I was your father didn't mean I could control your life."

Tony felt a wave of embarrassment sweep over him as he remembered that conversation from several years ago. Had he really sounded so arrogant and self-righteous?

"I can't believe I could have been so sanctimonious about everything," he muttered.

"Don't be too hard on yourself, Son. I had to admire the fact that you stood up to me, refused to be intimidated by anyone, even your father. That's why I've stayed out of your life unless you asked for my advice or help. I respect you, Tony, and respect your choices. You've done a good job making your life work for you."

Tony just shook his head, feeling more than a little sheepish. "It's a wonder you haven't lost patience with my belligerent attitude these past few years. I certainly haven't been the easiest person to be around, I know."

"All I'm saying is that there's nothing wrong with being independent, wanting to be on your own and enjoying a sense of your own accomplishments. You've got a considerable amount to be proud of, particularly because you did it on your own." Cole was quiet for several minutes before he asked, "Tell me, was Christina surprised when you asked her to marry her?"

"Flabbergasted. Acted like she'd never heard of the word. Especially where I'm concerned."

"Somehow, that doesn't surprise me. From everything I've heard you say about her, she's never considered the idea of marriage."

"Yeah. She can't imagine anyone wanting to marry her. Isn't that crazy?"

"At least you've given her something to think about."

"I doubt that. She couldn't say no fast enough."

"Because you caught her by surprise. Let's suppose that you allow her to leave, allow her to get on with whatever life she envisions without you. Meanwhile, you stay in touch with her, let her know that you still want to be friends, if nothing else. Give her some space, but don't drop out of her life entirely."

"Like you did with me?"

Cole grinned. "I didn't think you'd noticed."

Tony returned his father's grin with a lighter heart than he'd had since his painful conversation with Christina. Then he remembered something that caused his grin to fade.

"But once she testifies, she's going to have to go into some kind of a protection program. I won't know where she is or how to find her—"

"Do you recall our conversation awhile back—when I told you that if she decided not to marry you, I would make certain she got the help she needs?"

Tony nodded.

"Then we'll put that plan into action as soon as she's finished giving testimony at the trial. We'll let her decide where she wants to live. I'll help her get a place to stay and a job. Most important, she'll always know how to contact you. If she wants to get in touch with you, there won't be anything to stop her. You aren't a part of her old life."

"What if she doesn't want anything more to do with me?"

"Then you have to love her enough to respect her wishes. She hasn't had an easy life. She's struggled hard to get her education and make something of herself. She's used to taking her time to think things through and to decide what's best for her."

"You don't think I'm any good for her, do you?"

"I didn't say that. My thinking on the matter is this. Her life has been in total disruption for the past few months. She's had to live with strangers. I think she wants to get back to her home and belongings, even if they're located somewhere else. What I think is that she needs time. In this case, I would say time is on your side."

"How can you say that? Once she's gone, she'll forget all about me!"

"Just like you'll forget about her?"

"I love her!"

"How does she feel about you?"

"She said she loves me," he mumbled.

"So, she's going to set up her own life once again, find a routine and remember what life was like with you. She's going to remember going to sleep in your arms, waking up in your arms—"

"How did you know about..." Tony stopped, flushing.

"Because I know all about the connecting doors between those two bedrooms. That's my part of the house, remember?"

Tony dropped his chin on his chest. "Christina may be pregnant," he muttered.

Cole tensed. "She told you that?"

"No. But I got carried away in that hot tub last night and lost control."

A faint smile crossed Cole's lips. "Your sister Katie was conceived in that hot tub. It's amazing how history tends to repeat itself."

"But what if she is pregnant?"

"Give her the chance to tell you."

"If she doesn't?"

Cole's jaw hardened. "If she doesn't, then I will. I'll have her watched so closely that she won't be able to hide it."

"You'd do that for me, Dad?"

"I'd do it for the three of you. Like I said, there's some history that doesn't need to repeat itself. I've kept out of your affairs. But I find that I have to draw the line at the thought of not protecting a grandchild." He grinned at Tony. "The possibility of a grandbaby. Hot damn! Wouldn't that be something? Wait 'til I tell Allison."

Tony stiffened. "Dad! You can't tell Mom. She'll know that—"

"Tony, has it ever occurred to you that your mother might assume a thirty-year-old man has a normal sex life, particularly when he walked away from his prized ranch and rodeoing life-style to stay with a woman for three months?"

"But she never acted like—"

"Of course not. She was delighted to meet Christina, liked her immediately, but more important to both of us, liked to see the changes in you the young woman has caused. What you do in the privacy of your bedroom—or hers, or in that hot tub—is none of our business."

"I don't know what I would do without you, Dad," Tony said.

"Don't worry about it. You won't ever have to find out. I intend to stick around for a long, long time."

Six weeks later, Tony wearily mounted his porch steps and let himself into the dark house. The days were growing shorter, just when light was at a premium for him.

Hercules followed him into the house, his tail dragging. He was one tired hoss of a dog. He'd spent the day chasing rabbits and in general being a complete nuisance to the men who were building the heavily enforced corrals for the bulls they intended to bring in.

In the weeks since the trial and telling Christina goodbye, Tony had buried himself in his routine of hard work on the ranch, trying to put her out of his mind. He knew that his dad had been right. He didn't want Christina to stay in Texas and marry him if she felt that was her only choice. He only wanted her if she wanted him and his life-style.

He'd been impressed with the lengths to which the government people had gone to protect Christina. After meeting her in Washington, DC, the two men who had first interviewed her at the ranch accompanied her to Atlanta, where the federal case was tried.

Meanwhile, Cole began the careful process of having all of Christina's belongings packed up and moved, creating false paper trails and names that would confuse any would-be tracker.

Once her part in the trial was over, Christina met with government representatives as well as Cole to decide what she wanted to do and where she wanted to live. After taking a few days to consider, she chose to move to Portland, Oregon.

According to Cole, she'd taken a job as bookkeeper of a car dealership. The Treasury Department had suggested that she stay away from banks, just in case anyone attempted to trace her through her line of employment.

Cole, Christina and Tony had returned to Texas first to decide what she should do with the van and her animals. Cole had convinced her that she would be wise to leave the van and buy something new once she reached Portland. It was Cole who had suggested she interview with a man he knew who had a car dealership. He was certain she could get a good deal on a new car or van, as well.

Tony had watched her as she listened to the older man and considered his advice. She appeared calm throughout the discussion of her options, as though giving up her old life and friends was an accepted part of her existence.

The only time Tony saw her break down was when he offered to keep Hercules. It made sense to him that a dog that size should live in the country. She'd agreed that Hercules would be much better off on the ranch than in a small apartment, even if she could find an apartment complex that would accept an animal that big, which was doubtful.

She also understood the necessity of accepting Cole's offer to fly her to Portland in the company jet and help her get settled. At the moment, none of her identification could be used. The government had promised to prepare the necessary paperwork, giving her a new name and background as quickly as possible. In the meantime, Cole would ease her way into a new life.

Tony had gone to the airport to see them off.

Christina had kept any conversation between them very light. He hadn't pressed. Despite her outward appearance, he knew that she was shaken by recent events. It saddened him to think that his love for her had come as such a surprise, creating more stress in her life.

Cole went up to the front of the plane to speak to the pilot while Tony placed the cages holding Minerva and Prometheus in a place where they could see Christina.

He took her hand in his. "Let me hear from you, okay?" he said, clearing his throat of its sudden huskiness.

"Thank you for everything," she whispered. "You've treated me much more kindly than I deserve."

"You deserve much more than you seem to believe."

"I'll never forget our time together."

He forced himself to smile and say lightly, "I hope not."

"You deserve the very best that life has to offer."

"I found the best."

"Oh, Tony. Don't. You'll forget me soon enough."

He leaned down and gave her a very gentle kiss. When he lifted his head, he stared into her eyes. "Somehow I doubt it." Rather than make a complete fool of himself, he turned on his heel and left the plane.

In the six weeks she'd been gone, he hadn't heard anything from her. His father had kept him up-to-date on her life, which was how he knew about the apartment and the job. Cole told him that he and Allison had gotten into the habit of calling her on a weekly basis so that they could visit with her.

Tony knew that he could call her, but he hadn't. If she wanted to talk to him, she knew how to contact him. Besides, he couldn't think of anything casual to say to her. The gaping hole in his chest where his heart used to be had never healed. He wondered if it ever would.

On the brighter side of life, he'd had some fun calling Lin Schulz at the bank, thanking him for the offer of a loan and explaining that he didn't need it after all. He didn't bother to tell him that he'd discovered the interest he'd received on some of the lesser investments his dad had made for him was more than the original loan he'd requested.

It had been a strange feeling to realize that he'd been the one to let money stand between him and his father. He better understood what Cole had been trying to say about wealth. Having enough was fine; it made life comfortable. But having more than enough? It was just there, to be invested or worked or donated— whatever he chose to do with it. But it didn't change who he was.

Tony still loved the ranch. It felt good after a full day of hard physical labor to come home, knowing he'd accomplished something worthwhile. He looked forward to filling the giant tub he'd installed in his bathroom with hot water and lying there, soaking his weary bones.

Since Christina had come into his life, he'd learned to appreciate the small pleasures in his daily routine. She'd opened his eyes to so much that he'd been too busy to notice before.

Now, as he let himself into the house, he turned on the light, steeling himself to the sight of the brightly decorated kitchen. He certainly didn't need a reminder of Christina. She was never far from his thoughts.

It was funny what kept a person going. He looked after Hercules, knowing how much Christina loved the crazy mutt. It took only the first crack of thunder anymore and Tony prepared himself to help his poor, scared buddy through another traumatic experience.

Hercules was there for him, as well. We all have traumatic experiences to face from time to time, Tony thought to himself.

He checked Hercules's water bowl, refilled it, dumped dry food into another dish and opened a can of the moist stuff.

When he bent over to place the dish in front of Hercules, Tony groaned and rubbed his back. Boy, he was dragging tonight. They were really pushing him to get the corrals finished. He was eager to drive up to Fort Worth and pick up his new stock. Setting goals to work toward helped him to keep going.

He dug some leftovers out of the refrigerator and heated them up. Food didn't hold much interest to him these days. Consequently, he'd had to tighten his belt a couple of notches, and his jeans were beginning to hang on him.

The food had no taste, but he ate it anyway, then cleaned up the kitchen, turned off the light and headed for the bedroom. He was glad that he had never shared this bed with Christina, otherwise he couldn't have forced himself to sleep there at night.

Except to pick up Hercules, since she'd left he hadn't been back to the Circle C, but no one in the family found that unusual. Not with the self-imposed schedule he was keeping to.

He didn't wait for the tub to fill completely before he climbed in, groaning with the feel of the warm water on his tired body. He'd had to knock a bathroom wall out to install the thing, but it had been worth it.

He still toyed with the idea of building another home on the property. This house had been built in the twenties. The plumbing and wiring had been updated a couple of times, but there was a lot that needed to be done for real comfort. He might get around to building another place one of these days...or months...or years. Maybe, someday, when he was ready to look ahead at life rather than delving back into his past with a series of "what if's."

He'd been in the tub only a few minutes when the phone rang. Damn. He listened to it for a moment, debating whether to climb out and go answer it. Now he understood why his dad had a phone in every bathroom. Tony used to tease him about being decadent, but it would certainly make life a little easier.

He halfheartedly stirred, considering the need to answer, but then the phone stopped ringing. He relaxed back in the water. If it was important, they'd call back.

He didn't get many phone calls. He talked to his folks every week, but generally he called them. The steamy moisture began to work on his aching muscles. He leaned back in the tub and closed his eyes, letting his mind drift.

The ringing phone awakened him. Startled by the noisy intrusion, he flung himself out of the tub, splashing water onto the floor, and dashed to the phone before whoever was calling could hang up. He glanced at the clock, startled to see that he must have been asleep for almost an hour. Damn thing to do. He could have drowned.

He grabbed the phone and barked, "H'lo!"

"Tony?"

Dripping wet and without a towel, Tony sank down on the side of the bed, trying to draw some air into his lungs. The sound of Christina's voice had knocked all the wind out of him.

"Christina?" he asked, thinking he must be wrong.

"Did I call at a bad time?"

He glanced down at the rivulets of water trickling down his body. "Not really," he said, feeling himself start to smile like a fool. God, it was good to hear her voice! With a chuckle he said, "I was in the tub when the phone rang." A thought crossed his mind. "Is this the first time you've called?"

She hesitated before answering. "No. I called about an hour ago. I thought I'd try again. If you didn't answer this time, I'd know you'd gone somewhere for the evening."

"No, I'd just gotten into the tub and decided to ignore the phone. Then I ended up falling asleep. If you hadn't called, I might have spent the night in there!"

There was a long pause. Tony tried to think of something to say, but he was afraid of saying the wrong thing. So he remained silent, waiting to see why she had called.

Finally, Christina asked, "How have you been?"

He took a deep breath, concentrating on refilling his lungs before he attempted to answer. In a wry voice, he replied, "You want the truth or shall I be polite?"

"I always want the truth from you, Tony," she replied softly.

"You always get it." His mind was whirling with a jumble of feelings. There was so much he wanted to say, so much he was afraid to say. She wanted the truth. "Okay." He swallowed hard. "For whatever it's worth, I've been missing you like hell.'' He felt better just having said it out loud. With a little more confidence, he added, "There are times when I feel like all my insides have been ripped out and I'm dragging myself around half-dead." Was that honest enough for her? He brightened his voice very deliberately. "So. How have *you* been?"

"Oh, Tony," she whispered, her own voice breaking.

"Hey. I'm not trying to get sympathy.... Well, maybe a little. So tell me how you're doing. Do you like where you are...your job and apartment and everything?"

"I don't know who I'm most frustrated with at the moment, Minerva or your uncle Cody."

"Cody? What's he got to do with your life these days?"

"One thing he probably didn't know when he was playing his little joke was that a mynah bird mimics the voice as well as the saying. I recognized him immediately."

"Uh oh. I remember Cody mentioning something about teaching Minerva new phrases. What does she say?"

"A truly revolting singsong rendition, of 'Tony's in love with Christina, Tony's in love with Christina,' just like a little boy razzing another on the school grounds."

"I'm surprised it wasn't worse."

"It gets worse. There's also a very piercing, drawn-out wolf whistle and a comment about a pair of legs. Also a social comment about the color of my toenails...."

"You see what happens? The Callaways can easily corrupt the purest mind."

There was another long pause before she said, "I miss you, too, Tony."

He couldn't wipe the grin off his face. "I can't say I'm sorry to hear that."

"It's been so strange. I thought this move would be like all my other ones. I assumed that once I got settled and established a routine, my life would be like it has always been in the past. This time it's different. I keep thinking about you... and Hercules... and Texas... and wondering what's going on at the ranches. I think what I've been feeling is homesickness, or something similar. Isn't that ridiculous?"

"Not at all. I told you—we're your family now."

He heard a faint sound, as though she might be crying. He hated to think she was upset and all alone.

"Christina?"

"Yes?"

"How would you feel about my coming out to visit you?"

"Tony? Are you serious? Aren't you too busy to—"

He immediately dismissed the tight schedule he'd been keeping in order to get the stock moved to his ranch and said, "I could spare a couple of days. That is, if you wouldn't mind my coming out."

She laughed, but her voice trembled slightly. "I'd like very much to have you visit."

"Good! I mean, that's better than good. I'll call Dad and make arrangements to fly out. Is there anything I can bring?"

"I'd love to see Hercules, but the flight would scare him to death."

"Well, maybe you'll have to come to the ranch sometime to visit him."

There was another long pause before she said, "I'd like that, Tony. Very much."

Eleven

Tony hung up the phone and realized his jaw hurt from the wide smile that had been on his face since he'd discovered who was calling. He went back to the bathroom, grabbed a towel and finished drying himself off.

When he returned to the bedroom, he nudged Hercules with his foot. "Did you hear that, you lazy, good-for-nothing hound? She's misses us both. With your looks and my charm, we're going to coax her around to our way of thinking, just see if we don't."

Hercules lifted his head, sleepily blinked at Tony a couple of times, then sighed and returned to his exhausted slumber. He hid his excitement well.

Tony picked up the phone and called his dad to share the news and make plans to fly to the Pacific Northwest.

* * *

He recognized her by her untidy mop of reddish corkscrew curls. He'd caught a ride to the main terminal from the hangar where the plane would be waiting for his return flight. The crowded lobby didn't distract him in the least. He saw her right away.

"Christina?"

She whirled around at the sound of his voice. "Tony! There you are! I should have met you at the hangar, you know. There was no reason to have you come all this way just to—"

"It's good to see you," he said, interrupting her nervous chatter.

She burst out laughing and launched herself into his arms. He clutched her to him, silently vowing not to ever let her go so far from him again.

"Oh, Tony!" She pulled back and looked up at him, her hands cupping his jaws. "You've lost weight," she said accusingly.

"Probably." Who cared? He dipped his head and found her mouth. Oh, yes. This was the woman who had haunted him in memories and in dreams. His body responded as enthusiastically as his heart.

She pulled away from him. "Uh, Tony..." Her cheeks were flushed.

"Yeah, I know. You do seem to have that kind of an effect on me."

She glanced around at the milling people, most of whom were too busy with their own business to notice anyone else. "Are you ready to go home?"

His mouth twitched. "You could say that."

Her blush deepened and he laughed. The last few weeks were forgotten in the joy of being with her again. "C'mon and show me this new van you're driving these days." He wrapped his arm around her shoulders and they headed toward the parking area.

"Did you find a buyer for my old one?"

"Nope. Been driving it myself. Hercules is more comfortable in it."

"You take him with you?"

He brushed a kiss along her cheek. "Sure. He likes to go into town. He's got a regular following, you know. He's become the star of the county."

When they reached the new silver van, she handed him the keys. "I don't live far from here. I'm in northeast Portland."

Tony concentrated on following her directions. They got on the freeway and headed south and eventually took one of the exits east. She guided him to the apartment complex and her parking space, then took his hand and led him up the stairs.

He followed her into the apartment and stopped. The room was bright with color—yellows and greens, splashes of orange and gold—so that he felt he was on some South Seas island with all its tropical lushness.

White wicker furniture abounded, as did a multitude of plants. A familiar voice erupted from the bay window.

"'Praise the Lord!'"

"Well, hello, Minerva. It's good to see you, too."

A blur of yellow fur came flying across the floor and wrapped itself around his ankles. Tony knelt on one knee and scooped up the cat. "I'd swear that you recognize me," he said in amazement.

"Of course he recognizes you. He's very intelligent. I think he's missed you and Hercules."

Tony stood and walked over to one of the chairs. He sat down with the cat still in his arms. "I don't think my ego could handle discovering which of us you and Prometheus missed the most. I'll just be grateful I'm included."

"Are you hungry? I have something ready to pop into the oven."

"Sounds good. My appetite seems to be returning." He eyed her in her yellow ruffled blouse and gray slacks. "All of them," he muttered, still a little uncomfortable from his earlier reaction to her. "You're looking good, honey." What an understatement.

She walked over to the small kitchen area off the living room. "You look exhausted. You've been working too hard, haven't you?"

He shrugged and allowed Prometheus to stretch out along the length of his thigh. "Just trying to beat the bad weather."

After placing something in the oven and tossing a previously prepared salad, Christina brought him a glass of iced tea. "I'm surprised that you'd take any time off," she said, handing him the drink.

He took it, wrapping his fingers around hers so that she couldn't move away from him. "Seeing you was more important."

She sat down beside him. He released her hand so that he could drape his arm around her. He needed to touch her. He would always need to touch her; he'd learned that lesson very well these past few weeks.

"One of the things I need to do up front," she said, nervously twisting her fingers, "is to apologize for the way I behaved that last night at Cody's place."

"What do you mean?"

"The way I acted when you asked me to marry you. I didn't mean to be so insulting, as though being a Callaway was something bad. It's just that the Callaways are out of my league."

"We're just like anybody else, you know."

"Not really. Although, since I had time to think about everything, I realized that you yourself aren't wealthy. I mean, you went to the bank for a loan, just like most of us have to do. I was being silly, objecting to something over which you have no control. My only excuse was that I was so shocked you asked me to marry you that I wasn't thinking clearly. The whole idea really frightened me."

"So I gathered," he drawled.

"I think it was really good for me to move here. It gave me a chance to look at my life...and what I want from it."

He reached over, took one of her hands and placed it on his thigh. "There. I thought I'd give you something to do with your hand."

Hesitantly, she smoothed her fingers over the taut denim fabric that clung to his leg.

"I guess what I'm trying to say is . . ."

Tony tensed. He knew what he hoped she was trying to say. He was afraid to second-guess her. "Yes?"

She buried her head in his shoulder. "Oh, Tony. I love you so much it frightens me. I don't know what to do. I don't know how to be a wife. I've never thought I would want to be married. Once I left Texas, I tried to put the idea out of my head...but I couldn't."

He slipped Prometheus off his leg and gathered Christina onto his lap. She curled against him like a frightened child. He held her tightly, silently conveying that she was safe with him, there was no reason to be afraid.

"I, uh, know what you mean," he said after a few minutes. "I never figured on getting married myself. You think you don't know anything about being a wife? Well, look at me. I'm certainly not husband material, you know."

She raised her head until she could meet his gaze. "I think you could do anything you set your mind to."

"Funny. That's how I've always felt about you."

She gave him a kiss that he felt was reward enough for the emptiness of the last few weeks. When one kiss led to another, then one more, Tony felt his control slipping away.

He stood, still holding her, then placed her on the chair and walked across the room. He peered out the window, concentrated on his multiplication tables and recited the names of the presidents until his body calmed down enough for him to face her once more.

"Christina, I need to know something."

She watched him with a puzzled look on her face. "All right."

"Are you pregnant?"

Whatever she was expecting him to ask, that certainly wasn't it. She looked jolted and he mentally cursed his blunt approach. When she didn't respond immediately, he said, "It doesn't matter if you are, you know. I mean, I want to marry you. You know that. A baby would be a bonus."

"Is that why you think I called you?"

He shrugged. "I hadn't given it much thought. From the time you phoned and said you missed me, all

I've been able to think about was the possibility that you'd changed your mind about marrying me."

She sighed. "The answer to your question is, I don't know."

He crossed the room in a few strides and knelt beside her chair. "You mean there's a possibility you could be?"

She wouldn't meet his eyes. "I bought one of those home pregnancy tests a week ago, just to rule out the possibility. I haven't used it yet."

"Why not?"

"Because I'm not ready to know, one way or the other. My life seems so out of control already. Each day I kept hoping that I would... Then each evening I'd think about taking the test, but—"

He scooped her out of the chair and swung her around in a tight circle, laughing. "I'm glad you waited! I'm also glad I'm here. Christina, don't you understand? You aren't alone anymore. You've got me in your life, whether you like it or not. Plus, you've got the entire Callaway clan considering you as one of the family. If I could take away your lonely childhood, I would. The next best thing I can do is to provide you with a home and loved ones, and hopefully a family of our own."

She had slipped her arms around his neck when he'd grabbed her. Now she studied him from a few inches away. "You really wouldn't care, would you? I mean, if I happened to be pregnant."

The grin he gave her was definitely wicked. "If you aren't at the moment and I have any say in the matter, you will be shortly!"

"You really want to marry me, don't you?" she said with wonder in her voice.

"I believe I've pointed that out to you once or twice. Yeah. I want to marry you."

The oven buzzer went off, making them both jump.

Tony reluctantly allowed Christina to leave him long enough to turn off the oven. As soon as she turned around, he said, "For some reason, I'm not as hungry as I was awhile ago. I'd much prefer to rest for a while."

"Rest?" She eyed him doubtfully.

He nodded, full of innocence. "Before we rest, though, how about let's take that little test and see if we're going to be parents right away, okay?"

"Oh, Tony, I'm not sure that—"

"Don't worry. I'm sure enough for both of us. Fate wouldn't be so unkind as to have you walk into my life, let me fall in love with you, then have you walk away. I hope you are pregnant. I want you to learn to depend on me, to trust me, to let me love you."

She grinned and hugged him. "You Texans sure know how to woo a gal, I must say."

Then she took his hand and led him down the hallway to her bedroom.

Epilogue

Tony's back was sore from all the hard slaps he'd received recently from Cole, Cameron and Cody, but it didn't matter. All he could do was stand there grinning like a fool and loving every minute of it.

"Well, Grandpa," Cody said to Cole. "How's it feel to have a strapping eight pounder for a grandson?"

Cole angled the cigar between his teeth to point to the ceiling and smiled around it. "Nothing like it, bro. Nothing like it."

The four men were seated in Cole's den at his Austin home. They'd just left the hospital, after making certain that mother and son were resting comfortably for the night.

Tony was still feeling the strain of long hours in the labor and delivery rooms with Christina, entertaining her, coaching her, wiping the tears and perspiration away, promising never to do anything like this to her again and, finally, witnessing the arrival of his red-faced and angry young son.

He wouldn't have missed a second of it for the world.

His mother, Cameron's wife, Janine, and Carina had driven to San Antonio to check on their children, who had been left with Janine's housekeeper for the day. Tony had a hunch the woman would never be the same after that tribe got through with her.

Now he had a son to join in the confusion.

"I wonder when he's going to wipe that fool grin off his face?" Cameron asked no one in particular.

"Aw, leave him alone," Cole said with a suspiciously similar grin. "He deserves to gloat for a little while."

"It's funny how we take so much credit for something that we had so little to do with," Cody said, taking a puff on his cigar and blowing smoke rings.

"Our part may not take long, but it's a crucial part of the process," Tony pointed out.

"Not take long?" Cody repeated in a drawl. "Hell, Son. We're going to have to teach you a few things."

"He seems to have gotten the hang of things fine without your help," Cam said with a smile.

"You did fine, Son. Just fine."

"Thanks."

Tony rested his head on the back of his chair and closed his eyes. Lordy, he was tired. He hadn't been getting much sleep lately. Christina had been so uncomfortable these past few weeks. He'd gotten in the habit of sitting up with her, massaging her back or reading to her—whatever it took to get her mind off her condition.

She'd gotten upset when she could no longer see her feet, so he'd made quite a production one evening of placing her on the bed and carefully painting each of her toenails a different color so she would know her rainbow was still there.

The last months had been hectic, to say the least. He'd convinced Christina to fly back to Texas with him. When she'd called to explain to her boss, he'd been understanding. Tony found out later that Cole had already lined up another bookkeeper to take Christina's place in the event she decided to return to Texas.

Tony had hired movers to come in and pack everything for her, so that they were able to fly back right after she gathered some personal belongings together.

When they got home, Allison had been brimming with ideas for a quiet family wedding. Christina seemed relieved not to be expected to come up with plans. Allison had insisted that Christina stay in Austin until the big day, so Tony had returned to the ranch alone. However, he'd insisted on getting married almost immediately, despite all the plans his mother was suggesting. He smiled at the memory. He'd gotten his way, because Christina was eager to return to the ranch. Allison had laughingly agreed to having the wedding within a week.

The toughest part for him took place the morning after they returned to the ranch, after a short honeymoon on the Texas coast.

They were finishing breakfast. Tony took a sip of his coffee before he said, "I've been thinking about building another home here on the ranch."

"But why?" Christina looked around the kitchen. "What's wrong with this place?"

"Well, it's a little small for a family, don't you think? Having you decorate the kitchen made me realize how shabby the rest of the house has become. To be honest, I never paid much attention to the place. It was just somewhere to hang my hat and sleep. But now—now I want a place that you've helped to plan."

She eyed him uncertainly. "But, Tony, with a baby on the way, won't we have to be more careful with money? I won't be able to go back to work right away. With your loan at the bank and wanting to prove you can make the place work, maybe we should wait on building for a few years."

He reached for her hand, needing to touch her, praying that he would know how to explain what needed to be said.

"I know what you said about the Callaways—how you felt the income generated by the family businesses puts us in a different league. But that isn't true, not really. I mean, I will always want to work, Christina. That's part of who I am. The thing is, you need to know that I don't have to work. In fact, I ended up not taking that loan after all."

"I don't understand."

"Well, it seems that my dad, in all his wisdom, set aside my share of the company profits for several years without telling me. I can understand your distrust of wealth, because I felt that way myself for a long time. The thing that helped me to understand Dad's point of view was when I realized I didn't have to allow the money to come between me and the people I love. Money is a by-product, not the goal in life."

"It is to some people."

"But not to us, to you and me. Or to my family, for that matter. It's just there."

"So what you're saying is you have the money to build a house if you want."

"If *we* want. Any decisions will be made by both of us. I mean that. Whatever I have is yours. If you want to work once the baby's born, then we can make arrangements to have someone stay with him or her."

"Oh, no! I don't want someone else raising my baby, not if it isn't necessary."

"Then you can stay home and care for our child, and any others we might be fortunate enough to have."

"You really want to build a new place?"

He nodded. "I have some ideas that I'd like to show you. If we start building right away, we should have the place ready by the time the baby gets here."

Building the house had kept them busy. The completion date had become a race with the stork. However, they'd made it. He would be taking his wife and son to their new home.

Tony vaguely heard his dad and uncles joking with each other, swapping tales about their experiences as fathers. Their voices were fading away and he knew he was almost asleep, but it didn't matter.

Letting Christina walk out of his life had been the hardest thing he'd ever faced, but his dad had been right. He'd had to respect her need to look at her life and make the best choices for herself. However, he

hoped he never had to go through such a traumatic
experience again. He could only thank God that
Christina had wanted to marry him.

The baby was a bonus to help persuade her.

They brought the baby to her early in the morning.
The doctor had suggested she attempt to nurse him.
Now she was experiencing the tingling sensation of an
eager little mouth tugging at her breast.

"Your milk won't come in for another day or so,"
the nurse who'd brought him explained. "But he'll
still be getting nourishment from you."

Christina studied the tiny infant with awe. His hair
was thick and dark, but she'd been told the color could
change. His eyes were also dark and subject to change.
He looked so much like Tony. Her heart melted every
time she saw the resemblance.

Her son. She still had trouble at times believing that
she, Christina O'Reilly Callaway, was a mother and a
wife. She'd been too afraid of disappointment to
dream of a future like this one. She'd been content
with the life she'd made for herself without help from
others. However, the Callaways had shown her what
a little help and a lot of love could do to make her life
complete.

She could hardly wait to get back to the ranch.
They'd moved into the new house last week. She woke
up each morning with a sense of surprise at her good
fortune.

The rooms were open and airy, with lots of light
coming in from the wide windows and skylights. The
house sat on a knoll overlooking the rest of the ranch.
It was farther from the highway than the original

house, so that the noise from the stock pens didn't disturb them.

She glanced down and saw that the baby had fallen asleep. She lifted him to her shoulder as the nurse had shown her and gently rubbed his little back. He smelled so sweet. She understood much more about love and its many aspects now than she had a year ago. Her heart had stretched and expanded to encompass all these new feelings that she'd never known existed.

The nurse had returned the baby to the nursery when there was a soft tap on her open door. She glanced around and saw Cole Callaway standing there, hat in hand, wearing a huge grin. In his other hand was a giant flower arrangement, which he set down on the table beside the bed.

"I could have had these delivered," he said softly, as he leaned over and kissed her cheek, "but I wanted to have the chance to see you and let you know how proud I am of you. You've shown real grit...and courage. I couldn't love you more if you were my own daughter."

She squeezed his hand and blinked away the tears his words evoked. "That means a lot to me. Tony has always told me that the Callaways are my family. I thought I understood what he meant, but having a family means more to me with every day that passes."

"I peeked in on Jason Cole just now," he said, obviously pleased with his namesake. "He's sacked out, dead to the world." His eyes misted. "Tony's so proud of him. I have to laugh at his strutting."

"I've never gotten the chance to thank you for all your help when I was so confused about everything," she said. "Not only the financial part, which was considerable, but your emotional support, as well. You and Allison. You never made me feel that you judged me in any way. That meant so much to me at a time when my whole life was up in the air.''

"I knew you'd come around sooner or later. You're a smart woman. It was easy for me to see that you were in love with my son, even if you weren't as certain. It's a little easier to understand when you're watching from a distance. It gives a person some perspective.''

"Hey! What is this, sneaking in to see my woman when my back's turned?''

Cole straightened and looked over at his son. "You were as sound asleep when I peeked in on you this morning as that son of yours is right now. A real family resemblance there. So I decided to sneak away early and congratulate Christina on what a fine job she did.''

Tony leaned over and kissed his wife. "I agree,'' he whispered, pushing a wisp of hair away from her face. He didn't notice when Cole left the room.

"Can you believe this?'' he said. "You and me, parents? It boggles the mind.''

"We may have started off in life with not much in the way of families, but we've certainly made up for it since, wouldn't you say?''

The kiss he gave her was all the answer she needed.

* * * * *

JINGLE BELLS, WEDDING BELLS:
Silhouette's Christmas Collection for 1994

Christmas Wish List

*To beat the crowds at the malls and get the perfect present for *everyone,* even that snoopy Mrs. Smith next door!

*To get through the holiday parties without running my panty hose.

*To bake cookies, decorate the house and serve the perfect Christmas dinner—just like the women in all those magazines.

*To sit down, curl up and read my Silhouette Christmas stories!

Join *New York Times* bestselling author Nora Roberts, along with popular writers Barbara Boswell, Myrna Temte and Elizabeth August, as we celebrate the joys of Christmas—and the magic of marriage—with

JINGLE BELLS, WEDDING BELLS

Silhouette's Christmas Collection for 1994.

FREE TV 3268 DRAW RULES
NO PURCHASE OR OBLIGATION NECESSARY

COMING NEXT MONTH

Jilted!
They were left at the altar...
but not for long!

#889 THE ACCIDENTAL BRIDEGROOM—Ann Major
November's *Man of the Month* Rafe Steele never thought one night with
Cathy Calderon would make him a father. Now he had to find her before
she married someone else!

#890 TWO HEARTS, SLIGHTLY USED—Dixie Browning
Outer Banks
Frances Jones discovered the way to win sexy Brace Ridgeway was
through his stomach—until he got the flu and couldn't eat! But by then,
Brace only craved a sweet dessert called Frances....

#891 THE BRIDE SAYS NO—Cait London
Clementine Barlow gave rancher Evan Tanner a "Dear John" letter from
her sister, breaking their engagement. Even though the bride said no, will
this sister say yes?

#892 SORRY, THE BRIDE HAS ESCAPED—Raye Morgan
Ashley Carrington couldn't marry without love, so she ran off on her
wedding day. Was Kam Caine willing to risk falling in love to give this
former bride a chance?

#893 A GROOM FOR RED RIDING HOOD—Jennifer Greene
After being left at the altar, Mary Ellen Barnett knew she couldn't
trust anyone. Especially the wolf that lay underneath Steve Rawlings's
sexy exterior....

#894 BRIDAL BLUES—Cathie Linz
When Nick Grant came back home, Melissa Carlson enlisted his help to
win back her ex-fiancé. But once she succeeded, she realized it was Nick
she wanted to cure her bridal blues!

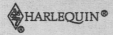 HARLEQUIN®   Silhouette®

The movie event of the season can be the reading event of the year!

Lights... The lights go on in October when CBS presents Harlequin/Silhouette Sunday Matinee Movies. These four movies are based on bestselling Harlequin and Silhouette novels.

Camera... As the cameras roll, be the first to read the original novels the movies are based on!

Action... Through this offer, you can have these books sent directly to you! Just fill in the order form below and you could be reading the books...before the movie!

48288-4	Treacherous Beauties by Cheryl Emerson		
		$3.99 U.S./$4.50 CAN.	☐
83305-9	Fantasy Man by Sharon Green		
		$3.99 U.S./$4.50 CAN.	☐
48289-2	A Change of Place by Tracy Sinclair		
		$3.99 U.S./$4.50CAN.	☐
83306-7	Another Woman by Margot Dalton		
		$3.99 U.S./$4.50 CAN.	☐

TOTAL AMOUNT	$	
POSTAGE & HANDLING	$	
($1.00 for one book, 50¢ for each additional)		
APPLICABLE TAXES*	$	_____
TOTAL PAYABLE	$	_____
(check or money order—please do not send cash)		

To order, complete this form and send it, along with a check or money order for the total above, payable to Harlequin Books, to: **In the U.S.:** 3010 Walden Avenue, P.O. Box 9047, Buffalo, NY 14269-9047; **In Canada:** P.O. Box 613, Fort Erie, Ontario, L2A 5X3.

Name: _____

Address: _____ City: _____

State/Prov.: _____ Zip/Postal Code: _____

*New York residents remit applicable sales taxes.
  Canadian residents remit applicable GST and provincial taxes.

CBSPR

"HOORAY FOR HOLLYWOOD" SWEEPSTAKES

HERE'S HOW THE SWEEPSTAKES WORKS

OFFICIAL RULES — NO PURCHASE NECESSARY

To enter, complete an Official Entry Form or hand print on a 3" x 5" card the words "HOORAY FOR HOLLYWOOD", your name and address and mail your entry in the pre-addressed envelope (if provided) or to: "Hooray for Hollywood" Sweepstakes, P.O. Box 9076, Buffalo, NY 14269-9076 or "Hooray for Hollywood" Sweepstakes, P.O. Box 637, Fort Erie, Ontario L2A 5X3. Entries must be sent via First Class Mail and be received no later than 12/31/94. No liability is assumed for lost, late or misdirected mail.

Winners will be selected in random drawings to be conducted no later than January 31, 1995 from all eligible entries received.

Grand Prize: A 7-day/6-night trip for 2 to Los Angeles, CA including round trip air transportation from commercial airport nearest winner's residence, accommodations at the Regent Beverly Wilshire Hotel, free rental car, and $1,000 spending money. (Approximate prize value which will vary dependent upon winner's residence: $5,400.00 U.S.); 500 Second Prizes: A pair of "Hollywood Star" sunglasses (prize value: $9.95 U.S. each). Winner selection is under the supervision of D.L. Blair, Inc., an independent judging organization, whose decisions are final. Grand Prize travelers must sign and return a release of liability prior to traveling. Trip must be taken by 2/1/96 and is subject to airline schedules and accommodations availability.

Sweepstakes offer is open to residents of the U.S. (except Puerto Rico) and Canada who are 18 years of age or older, except employees and immediate family members of Harlequin Enterprises, Ltd., its affiliates, subsidiaries, and all agencies, entities or persons connected with the use, marketing or conduct of this sweepstakes. All federal, state, provincial, municipal and local laws apply. Offer void wherever prohibited by law. Taxes and/or duties are the sole responsibility of the winners. Any litigation within the province of Quebec respecting the conduct and awarding of prizes may be submitted to the Regie des loteries et courses du Quebec. All prizes will be awarded; winners will be notified by mail. No substitution of prizes are permitted. Odds of winning are dependent upon the number of eligible entries received.

Potential grand prize winner must sign and return an Affidavit of Eligibility within 30 days of notification. In the event of non-compliance within this time period, prize may be awarded to an alternate winner. Prize notification returned as undeliverable may result in the awarding of prize to an alternate winner. By acceptance of their prize, winners consent to use of their names, photographs, or likenesses for purpose of advertising, trade and promotion on behalf of Harlequin Enterprises, Ltd., without further compensation unless prohibited by law. A Canadian winner must correctly answer an arithmetical skill-testing question in order to be awarded the prize.

For a list of winners (available after 2/28/95), send a separate stamped, self-addressed envelope to: Hooray for Hollywood Sweepstakes 3252 Winners, P.O. Box 4200, Blair, NE 68009.

CBSRLS

OFFICIAL ENTRY COUPON

"Hooray for Hollywood"
SWEEPSTAKES!

Yes, I'd love to win the Grand Prize — a vacation in Hollywood —
or one of 500 pairs of "sunglasses of the stars"! Please enter me
in the sweepstakes!

This entry must be received by December 31, 1994.
Winners will be notified by January 31, 1995.

Name _____

Address _____ Apt. _____

City _____

State/Prov. _____ Zip/Postal Code _____

Daytime phone number _____
(area code)

Mail all entries to: Hooray for Hollywood Sweepstakes,
P.O. Box 9076, Buffalo, NY 14269-9076.
In Canada, mail to: Hooray for Hollywood Sweepstakes,
P.O. Box 637, Fort Erie, ON L2A 5X3.

KCH

OFFICIAL ENTRY COUPON

"Hooray for Hollywood"
SWEEPSTAKES!

Yes, I'd love to win the Grand Prize — a vacation in Hollywood —
or one of 500 pairs of "sunglasses of the stars"! Please enter me
in the sweepstakes!

This entry must be received by December 31, 1994.
Winners will be notified by January 31, 1995.

Name _____

Address _____ Apt. _____

City _____

State/Prov. _____ Zip/Postal Code _____

Daytime phone number _____
(area code)

Mail all entries to: Hooray for Hollywood Sweepstakes,
P.O. Box 9076, Buffalo, NY 14269-9076.
In Canada, mail to: Hooray for Hollywood Sweepstakes,
P.O. Box 637, Fort Erie, ON L2A 5X3.

KCH